Pride Publishing books by Bailey Bradford

Single Books
Breaking the Devil
Dark Nights and Headlights
Texas and Tarantulas
Belt Buckles and Cowboy Boots
Something Shattered
Yes, Forever
The Jasper Soul

Southwestern Shifters
Rescued
Relentless
Reckless
Rendered
Resilience
Reverence
Revolution
Revenge
Reluctance
Renounced
Retrograde

Southern Spirits
A Subtle Breeze
When the Dead Speak
All of the Voices
Wait Until Dawn
Aftermath
What Remains
Ascension
Whirlwind

Love in Xxchange
Rory's Last Chance
Miles To Go
Bend
What Matters Most

Ex's and O's
A Bit of Me
A Bit of You
In My Arms Tonight
Where There's a Will
My Heart to Keep

Leopard's Spots
Levi
Oscar
Timothy
Isaiah
Gilbert
Esau
Sullivan
Wesley
Nischal
Justice
Sabin
Cliff

Mossy Glenn Ranch
Chaps and Hope
Ropes and Dreams
Saddles and Memories
Fences and Freedom
Riding and Regrets
Broncs and Bullies
Hay and Heartbreak
Vaqueros and Vigilance

Spotless
Hide
Hunt
Home
Heart

Mystic Tattoos
One Too Many

Coyote's Call
Off Course
In from the Cold
Blue Moon Rising

Valen's Pack
Run with the Moon
Exodus

The Vamp for Me
My Life Without Garlic
Don't Stake My Life on It
Sunshine is Overrated
Don't Drink the Holy Water
The Trouble with Mirrors
That's One Cross Vamp

Power
Exchange
Submit
Dominate

Calendar Men
Mr. January
Mr. February
Mr. March
Mr. April
Mr. May
Mr. June
Mr. July
Mr. August
Mr September
Mr. October
Mr. November
Mr. December
The 13th Month

City Shifters
Bearly There
Harey Situation

Mossy Glenn Ranch
Chaps and Hope
Ropes and Dreams
Saddles and Memories
Fences and Freedom
Riding and Regrets
Broncs and Bullies
Hay and Heartbreak
Vaqueros and Vigilance

Fire and Flutter
Dragon Dreams and Fairy Wings

Wild Ones
Destined Prey

Intrinsic Values
Artifacts

Anthologies
What's his Passion?: Unexpected Places
What's his Passion?: Unexpected Moments
Racing Hearts: The Lonely Ones

Intrinsic Values

ARTIFACTS

BAILEY BRADFORD

Artifacts
ISBN # 978-1-83943-970-4
©Copyright Bailey Bradford 2021
Cover Art by Claire Siemaszkiewicz ©Copyright April 2021
Interior text design by Claire Siemaszkiewicz
Pride Publishing

Published in 2021 by Pride Publishing, United Kingdom.

Pride Publishing is an imprint of Totally Entwined Group Limited.

ARTIFACTS

Dedication

To everybody who's ever had difficulty being accepted for what you are. What y'all are is amazing.

Chapter One

The *Help Wanted* sign in the window stopped Aldric in his tracks. He'd been walking along San Antonio's Pearl District, somewhat lost in his thoughts and worries, so why he noticed the sign, he couldn't have said.

Maybe because it stood out in the day of internet-everything. All the job boards that he'd scanned and the applications for employment that he'd sent in had been online. That was just how it was done nowadays...except not at the business he'd stopped in front of.

Aldric stared at the sign for a solid minute while trying to calculate his chances of being hired if he went in and applied before going home and changing. Not that he had any fancier clothes. Jeans, T-shirts and one button-up were all that was in his wardrobe.

What are the chances someone else will apply and get hired by the time I go home, shower, shave, change and come back?

Whatever the odds were, his empty stomach didn't want to risk them. Blinking away his musings, Aldric pushed his glasses farther up his nose, then caught himself screwing up his face to re-settle them exactly where they'd been. He attempted to smooth down his hair—being thick, it tended to tousle, even though it wasn't long—and reached for the door handle, which was when he saw the name of the place that was hiring.

Intrinsic Value Antique Shop. At least shop wasn't spelled all funky. It was a silly pet peeve he had, people adding extra letters onto words to make spellings like *shoppe* rather than shop. An antique store might have a better reason than most businesses or services to use an old spelling of the word, and he had no reason to be judgmental of anything—something he needed to keep in mind.

Even though he knew nothing about antiques, Aldric opened the door and stepped inside to the tinkling of chimes. He glanced down at the door handle inside and saw strings of silver and copper bells dangling from it.

"Good afternoon. May I help you?"

Aldric pivoted so quickly that he almost tripped over his own feet—nothing unusual for him. Heat rushed to his face, and he gulped as he spotted the older man standing with one hand on an ancient-looking cash register. "Er, yes, I, um, I—" Aldric took a deep breath and exhaled to the count of ten. If he didn't get himself calmed down, he'd stumble over his words as well as his feet, as he tended to do when he was flustered.

"My name is Elliot Douglas. I'm the owner of Intrinsic Value. Please call me Elliot." Elliot came around the counter and stopped in front of Aldric.

"Aldric Beamer." Aldric offered his right hand to shake. "Nice to meet you, Elliot." His mouth was dry, and a tickle started up in his throat.

"Nice to meet you, too." Elliot pumped his hand one more time, then let go. "Are you here about the job? I noticed you standing outside and thought you might be considering it."

Aldric covered his mouth and turned his head before he coughed. He lowered his hand and faced Elliot again. "Sorry, the mountain cedar is kicking my allergies into high gear. Yes, sir, I'm here about the job. Surprised me to see an actual sign in the window. Everything's done online, it seems. I've been told to go home and apply online so often, I've quit thinking about actual signs."

"Ah yes, the internet is an amazing tool for many things, but I prefer to meet people in person first, rather than online." Elliot smiled, and Aldric realized the older, taller man, with his tawny-brown eyes and thick mane of slightly long, wavy light-brown hair that was just starting to silver, was quite handsome.

"Why don't you come back this way and tell me what makes you think you'll be a good fit at Intrinsic Value?" Elliot gestured in the direction of the cash register. "I was cleaning off my baby and would like to finish as we talk."

"Yes, sir." Aldric coughed again and wanted to melt into the floorboards.

"Would you like some cold water or hot tea?" Elliot offered. "I have both available."

Aldric wasn't sure about hot tea. He'd only ever had Texas tea—cold, with lots of sugar and ice in it. But maybe tea was a thing with Elliot. "Er, tea, please?"

Elliot glanced back at him. "You sound uncertain. Have you tried hot tea before?"

Lying wasn't something Aldric did if he could help it. "I haven't, but I thought a warm drink might help with my scratchy throat."

"That it might. I have a few different kinds, but how about you try the chamomile? It's good for all sorts of ailments." Elliot stopped by an elegant-legged wooden table that had a silver tea kettle and several mismatched cups and saucers sitting on it.

A white ceramic dish held glass jars of tea and cubes of sugar, and a clear container was filled with what appeared to be honey. Delicate silver spoons were laid out as well. Aldric tucked his hands into the front pockets of his jeans. Everything on that table looked delicate, not only the spoons, and he was afraid to touch anything.

Which had to mean he shouldn't apply for the job.

"Aldric?" Elliot arched one thick eyebrow. "Is chamomile okay?"

Realizing he'd more than likely made sure he wouldn't get hired, because Elliot had to think he was on the dense side, Aldric shook his head. "It's okay, thank you. I'll just—" He started to take a step back.

"Just what?" Elliot asked, scooping tea from a jar before he put it into a little oval-shaped strainer. "Are you not interested in the job after all?"

Aldric bit his bottom lip and pondered whether he should stay or not. For one thing, he'd already made some kind of impression, good or bad. For another, Elliot hadn't run him off. *That has to mean I still have a chance, right? Until I tell him I know nothing about what this shop sells. Damn it.*

"I'm interested, but I don't have any experience with antiques," Aldric rushed out, watching Elliot pour hot water over the strainer holding the tea. Elliot had put a lid on it so the tea leaves didn't flow out.

Aldric took a step closer, unable to resist getting a better look at what Elliot was doing. He took off his round-framed glasses, polished them and shoved them back on.

"The tea needs to steep for a few minutes," Elliot explained. "The infuser keeps most of the bits of tea leaves from escaping, but you still might have a few pieces in your cup. Those will usually settle at the bottom."

"That's the infuser?" Aldric asked when Elliot nudged the strainer holding the tea.

Elliot smiled at him. "Yes, it is. Do you like honey?"

"I—" Aldric's stomach picked that moment to let out a rumbling growl. He dropped his gaze and pressed a fist to his belly. "Sorry. Skipped breakfast."

"Well, that won't do. It's almost time for dinner. I'll order us something to eat, then you and I will sit down for a proper interview—if you're interested in the job?" Elliot picked up the jar of honey.

"Oh, I...I am, I just thought I'd blown any chance I had at it." Aldric ducked his head and stared at the worn toes of his tennis shoes. "I don't have any experience for it. I've only worked at fast-food places. I don't know anything about antiques. I didn't even know what that thing—the infuser—was." His ignorance was embarrassing, and he hated that he didn't know more.

"So," Elliot drawled, one corner of his mouth curving up. "No experience at all? That would mean I'd have a clean slate in you, if I were to hire you. Wouldn't have to rid you of bad habits and misinformation."

Aldric was almost too afraid to believe he might have a chance of keeping his shitty apartment and not going hungry for much longer, after all. "Are you serious?"

"Utterly. Here, let me fix your tea, then I'll order something from the restaurant across the street. It has a little of everything. I have a menu for it behind the counter. This won't take a moment..." Elliot took the infuser out, then added honey to the tea.

"Thank you." Aldric should have refused the offer of a meal, but the truth was, he was too hungry to let pride cost him sustenance. He took the warm cup of tea from Elliot and inhaled the fragrant steam rising from it. "Oh! This smells good."

Elliot smiled at him, a delighted expression, if Aldric wasn't reading him wrong. "I hope you'll like the way it tastes as well. Let me grab that menu, then you can peruse it with me."

"Okay, thanks." Aldric took a sip of the tea. It was hotter on his tongue than he'd expected, and he winced as he swallowed. He was glad Elliot hadn't seen him do that. The next sip he took was slower. The taste was as pleasant as the smell of the tea, the honey sweet but not overpowering.

"Here we go. I haven't had anything bad from here yet, but then again, I always order the same thing. I'm a creature of habit in many ways." Elliot's smile had turned rueful.

"What do you get?" Aldric asked before taking another drink. He could get addicted to hot tea.

"Nothing adventurous, just the grilled salmon with steamed vegetables and mashed sweet potatoes." Elliot handed him the menu. "I think the burgers should be good, though. Whenever I'm in the restaurant and see and smell them, they remind me very much of the ones my brother used to love."

"Younger or older brother?" Aldric flipped the paper menu open to scan the selections.

Elliot froze for a second, as though something were wrong. Before Aldric could ask him if he was okay, Elliot drew in a breath, then touched his temples, where he had a few strands of gray. "Younger. Chris is thirty-two, Natty is thirty-four and I'm the old man at forty-something. Do you have any siblings?"

Aldric decided he'd get the bacon burger and sweet potato fries. He'd never had the latter before. "I have two, like you. Twins. They're almost twenty years older than me."

Elliot's eyes widened. "That's two whole decades!"

"Yeah. I was a surprise," Aldric muttered. That was a nicer description than his family had called him at times. "Gregory and Simon are forty. I'm twenty-one." He hoped Elliot wouldn't ask any more questions about them, or Aldric's family, period. Hoping to avert such possibilities, Aldric tapped the menu. "Can I get this? The bacon-mushroom burger?"

"Of course, of course." Elliot moved back behind the counter and picked up something black. He stuck one finger in a silver ring that had smaller holes in it, and it took Aldric a moment to realize Elliot was using some kind of old phone.

Aldric had vague memories of his parents having a landline, but by the time he'd been old enough to care about it, they'd had cell phones. Even so, none of the phones Aldric had ever seen had looked like the one Elliot was now speaking into.

Elliot grinned as if he knew what Aldric was thinking, making Aldric look away and take another drink of his tea. When Elliot had looked at him then, it had occurred to Aldric that his potential boss was not only quite handsome, but very attractive. *He's about the same age as my brothers, so gross.* Aldric needed a job more than he needed to get laid, and he'd never been attracted to older men, either—and he wasn't about to start down that road now.

Not that Elliot would be interested in someone like him. Even though he'd only spent fifteen minutes in Elliot's presence, Aldric could already tell that the guy was much classier than he'd ever be. There was also the very real possibility that Elliot wasn't gay, despite the vibes Aldric was reading. Well, it didn't matter one way or another.

Elliot hung up and tapped the black phone. "It's an ancient rotary phone. My grandparents and parents had these, way back when, although we'd upgraded to a push-button phone by the time I started school. Want to see how it works?"

Aldric was itching to do just that. "Yeah, I mean, yes, I'd like that."

The lesson taught him more than how to dial out on the phone—it taught him that Elliot was a patient and kind man. He encouraged and answered any questions Aldric had, which was freeing in a way that Aldric hadn't experienced before. The old saying about children being seen but not heard had been a rule in his parents' home.

"You have an inquisitive nature and a good brain." Elliot propped a hip against the counter. "I think you'll do well here."

Aldric blinked in surprise. He was glad he'd set the teacup down, or else he might have dropped it, considering how much his hands trembled. "I have the job?"

Elliot nodded. "You do."

"But…what about references and work history?" Aldric regretted asking as soon as the words were spoken.

"I like to believe I have excellent judgment when it comes to people," Elliot said. "Am I wrong in regard to you?"

Aldric shook his head. "No. It's just, I don't know anything about antiques, or what I'll be doing."

"You can learn. Someone gave me a chance a few years ago and made this" — Elliot swept a hand toward the antiques in the shop — "possible. I'm still learning, one might say. That's one reason I keep alphabetized cards on every item in the store, as well as those in the back. If someone asks about, say, this…" Elliot walked over to the second row of shelves and pointed to a silver tray. "What does it look like to you?"

Sweat broke out on Aldric's brow. He knew what the object looked like to *him*, and it seemed obvious — was Elliot trying to trick him? No, Elliot had been nothing but kind to him. Aldric couldn't let his own insecurity get the better of him now. "A-a silver tray?"

Elliot's smile could have lit up the room. "Yes! So you'd just open the gold-leafed book under the register — go ahead and find it. Open it and look up 'silver tray'."

Aldric did as directed and was delighted to discover that most of the cards also had a small image of the item on the right corner. "It's an eighteenth-century silver salver." He read off the rest of the information, relief coursing through him even as he stumbled over some of the words. He could do this job.

"You won't be alone in the store often, not at first," Elliot said. "I'll be out on the floor with you or, once you've been here for a while, in my office. Sometimes I'm away for a day or so, for instance at a fair or auction, or I might have to leave the city, to procure or sell an antique or attend an event, but I close the shop then."

Aldric's excitement fizzled out. "Oh. How…how long would you be gone? How often does that happen?" He'd lose out on work, and if he couldn't support himself —

"I'd have you come in and work in the back while I'm gone. There will always be plenty of cleaning that can be done. I'll show you how to polish silver and clean antiques — the ones that should be cleaned," Elliot added before the door opened, and a young woman carrying a box entered. "Meredith! You are an angel of mercy."

Meredith shook her head, making her brown hair ruffle over her shoulders, and chuckled. "Hardly. I'm just the delivery chick from across the street. Who's this?"

"Aldric Beamer, my new employee," Elliot answered, glancing at Aldric. "Right?"

"He's not sure?" Meredith asked before Aldric could answer. She winked at him. "You should work for Mr. Douglas. He's cool, and I bet he pays well, judging by the tips he gives me."

Aldric hadn't even thought to ask what his wages would be. The whole job-thing had happened so fast it felt like a dream.

"We haven't discussed his pay." Elliot took out his wallet and removed several bills from it. "But, of course, I believe in paying a livable wage."

Aldric knew first-hand that minimum wage wasn't a livable wage. He'd worked just under full-time and had often skipped meals to make rent. More than once, his electricity had been cut off. No fast-food joint he'd worked at had wanted to employ him full-time — that would have meant offering him health insurance. Then things had taken a turn for the worse and he'd found himself unemployed and hovering at the edge of homelessness.

"Aldric?"

Aldric lifted his glasses with one hand and rubbed a knuckle of the other into his eye. "Sorry. I sort of drifted off. I promise I won't do that while I'm on the clock."

Elliot held out a box and a drink. "I have utter faith in your ability to work well. Here, take this and head to the back. Second door on the left is my office. We'll dine in there."

"Fancy," Meredith said, her brown eyes alive with humor. "Nice meeting you, Aldric."

"Nice meeting you, too," he replied, his face heating because he'd mentally checked out in front of her and Elliot.

He found Elliot's office and was almost afraid to sit down in the plush leather chairs. The whole room looked like something out of an old-time movie, with its shiny wood surfaces, smooth leather seats and framed black-and-white photos from decades ago on the walls.

"Have a seat. Well, scoot closer to the desk if you want to use it for a table." Elliot came around to the other side of his desk and sat, placing his own food on it. "There's a coaster for your drink in the wood tray to your left."

Aldric found the coaster and set his drink and boxed meal down before moving one of the leather chairs closer. "This is a very nice office. Is everything in it antique?"

Elliot began removing his food from the box it had come in. "Yes, except the pens and paper. Although I do have a quill pen!" He pointed at a long white feather. "It's not quite an antique, but I like it."

Aldric took a bite of his burger, and his stomach gave a happy rumble. "This is good," he muttered after he'd swallowed.

Elliot grinned. "I'm glad you like it. My salmon smells amazing, as always. Before I start in on it, though, I want to cover salary, hours and health insurance."

Aldric almost choked on the sweet potato fry he'd just bitten into. "Health insurance?" *No.* His ears were playing tricks on him.

But they weren't. Elliot explained how he'd make sure Aldric was covered, without a waiting period. Aldric would have a full forty hours a week, would be paid at time and a half for any hours over that, and while he wouldn't get rich working at Intrinsic Value, he'd earn that much-longed-for livable wage. It seemed too good to be true, and Aldric quickly and gratefully accepted everything he was offered, hoping that nothing happened to make this dream-come-true come crashing down around him.

Chapter Two

Officer Darrell Williams stared straight ahead as Sergeant Fuentes spoke...and spoke a little more, then more still. He tried not to catch his partner's eye, even when Sean O'Hara shifted his weight from one foot to the other. *Especially then.* It meant Sean would be rolling his eyes and giving a jerk of his red head in their sergeant's direction.

"And they say *my* people have the gift of the gab," Sean muttered out of the side of his mouth, putting on an Irish lilt he didn't have in real life.

Darrell shot a quick look from the corners of his eyes around the substation's press briefing room to check if anyone else had heard. The detectives wouldn't have, being on Fuentes' other side, for all they and uniform were sharing the same stage at the front of the room. The division between the two branches persisted in media conferences as in life. He didn't begrudge his sergeant, or any of them, their moment in the spotlight. He just wished he didn't have to be in it too. Especially with the way Fuentes was gearing up for the end of the story.

"Vigilance, surveillance, perseverance." Sergeant Fuentes repeated his mantra and nodded at Officer Laurie Strauss to switch to the next slide. This one got a little gasp, mainly from the members of the public who were part of the Civilian Involvement Program, rather than the reporters present, all sitting on the regulation hard plastic chairs. Darrell didn't look at the screen, instead keeping his gaze directed at the back of the room. At the wall, not at anyone who was attending this for him. It was impossible to do that, because no one *was* there for him.

Although he could appreciate Fuentes' skill in storytelling, making the bust sound dramatic, Darrell tuned out the description of that night. He had no need to hear it—he'd been there. And now, as a result, he was here.

"Officers O'Hara and Williams are especially commended..."

Darrell closed his ears more firmly at that, giving a tight nod at the gesture pointing him out as he stood there in all his five-feet-nine crew-cut glory, his arms by his sides, eyes front, face blank, at attention. Sean was no doubt offering up a cheesy grin, mainly to his steady girlfriend, who'd come to watch him today, and on whom he routinely cheated, mainly with Laurie Strauss.

Darrell was well aware of what he'd done. His job, making sure San Antonio had one less offshoot of the Mexican Mafia running its streets...at least for a while.

His actions had been simple enough in themselves. As a result of the team's vigilance and surveillance, to quote their sergeant, not to mention the stake-out, he'd gone into the Casa Hernandez restaurant to serve a minor citation…when the mafia boss had been holding a meeting. The La eMe leader, Ramon 'Rapido' Estrada, had ordered his lieutenant Felix 'El Gato' to pay Darrell off, then, when Darrell had refused the money, had ordered him to *"see him off"*, which was when The Cat had gone for his gun. Darrell had beaten him to the draw—his speed was probably the reason he'd been chosen for the assignment. Anyway, it had allowed the SWAT team to storm in.

Whoops and cheers greeted the footage of the raid. Darrell didn't join in with them, or grin at his family cheering on his behalf. He couldn't. None of them, his father or brothers, were among the audience. A small, tight smile took up some room on his face at the adjectives being used to describe his heroism. "Bravery," he heard. Pity he didn't agree with it.

"Officer Williams?" his sergeant said. Or repeated, Darrell realized, when Fuentes raised an eyebrow at him and gave a head tilt at a kid with his hand raised. The Civilian Involvement Program included high school students.

"Yes." Darrell pointed at the boy, for him to go ahead and ask his question.

"So you just walked into that restaurant during that meeting, with a bullshit—"

"Tyler!" snapped the adult two seats down.

"Sorry. B…ogus complaint," the kid continued.

"Wasn't b…ogus." Darrell addressed the boy. "Someone really had parked in front of a fire hydrant."

"Okay, and you knew he'd just bribe you?" Tyler asked.

"Try. Try to bribe me," Darrell corrected again.

"Didn't you think he'd attack you?" asked the girl to Tyler's left, as if taking up the baton for him. Maybe each kid was only allowed one question and Tyler had already stretched the rules. He looked the sort of kid who considered rules to be flexible.

"Thought he'd try. I mean, there was a strong possibility of it, when we ran the scenarios, based on—"

"Vigilance, surveillance," came from Sean, on a fake cough.

"Profiles built up of the gang members." Darrell ignored Sean and indicated the detectives on the low platform, with all their myriad roles and specializations.

"*Attack*? That psycho tried to *kill* you, man!" called another kid, who received a snapped-out, "Diego! You are in a police station!" for his remark. "Sorry. That psycho tried to kill you, *Officer*."

"Again, a possibility." Darrell stood straighter.

The girl raised her hand. "Could we see it again?"

Several voices, teenager and adult, added their support to the request, and this time, when the video — a mix of various cam feeds from the restaurant—ran, Darrell watched too, seeing El Gato fake-telegraph throwing a punch with one hand but really going for his gun with the other, and screen-Darrell pivot, as if attempting to get out of fist range, but really drawing his own weapon, beating the gang member to it.

They'd learned through surveillance that at those meetings, only the lieutenants carried firearms, with everyone else made to leave theirs on a table at one end of the room, so in theory, the risk of someone firing off a round at him had been minimal—but in practice, any of the gang could have had a gun tucked away and been trigger happy, wanting to get in with the boss. But they hadn't. Or hadn't had time. Which amounted to the same thing.

A shaven-headed guy raised a hand, showing his full tatt sleeve. "Your reaction, that move — that MMA? Or some specific martial art, to get that awareness and speed?"

Now a smile did cross Darrell's face, although it was bittersweet. "A mix, yeah, in that I grew up with two brothers, one older, and who both knew as soon as they could talk they wanted to go into the military, like Dad."

When the chuckles died down, Fuentes explained, "Officer Williams' father, Major Williams, is a Silver Star Medal decorated Special Reconnaissance Battlefield Airman of the United States Air Force Special Operations Command, now back here at Lackland AFB after distinguished active service. He designed and still runs the Special Warfare Preparatory Course and the Assessment and Selection Course, training future Special Reconnaissance operators, both sections of which have an attrition rate of almost ninety-five percent."

This got applause. "And Officer William's elder brother is now part of the Special Operations Aviation Regiment," Fuentes continued. "Who knows what that is?"

"Night Stalkers!" called the tattooed guy, punching the air, although Fuentes had probably been asking the high schoolers.

And my younger brother is now at Randolph AFB. Darrell wondered if Fuentes would add that too. If he did, Darrell missed it, because he'd tuned out again.

"Dazzle. Top brass alert."

Darrell snapped to at his partner's nickname for him and his warning that the captain was there. Sean stood by his side and Captain Miller opposite them, his hand outstretched and his body angled away, so the cameras could get a shot of him shaking hands with and congratulating his two officers.

"Honey!" Daniela, Sean's girlfriend, rushed up as soon as Miller moved on, grabbing Sean's hand. "You looked so good up there!"

"It's the uniform." Darrell gave the standard reply. "Hi, Dani." He bent down to receive her kiss on the cheek and hoped her perfume, something heavy and floral, didn't rub off on him.

Daniela prodded him. "Darrell, there's no one special here for you? You know, it's time you came out with me and Sean and one of my girlfriends again. Don't you think he'd like Ava?" she asked Sean.

"What's not to like?" Sean's reply earned him a slap to his arm. "Darrell?"

That note to Sean's voice, that seemed to make the question stretch, or deepen... Was it an invitation? Did Sean want Darrell to talk about why none of the *chicas* did it for him, why he hadn't been interested in Madison, the last friend Daniela had rustled up for him, and wouldn't be into Ava or, in all probability, any girl Daniela or Sean produced? Darrell wished he could. Wished he could talk openly about his sexuality. The thought of telling his father brought a bitter scratch of a laugh to his throat.

"I have to call Ryan," he invented. "He couldn't make it."

"Basic training, right." Daniela nodded. San Antonio was called Military City USA for a reason. She, like everyone who'd grown up there, understood. "Bet he's proud of his big brother, huh? Like Sean's are of him?"

Darrell was lucky—the photographer from the *San Antonio Chronicle* approached Sean, or actually, Sean and Daniela, for a picture, and saved him answering. Getting into position to show off her best features took all Daniela's attention, so Darrell slipped out of the room and around a corner, into a quieter spot, away from phones ringing, doors buzzing and keys jingling. He took out his phone and scrolled through his contacts, but didn't get as far as *R* for his brother Ryan. His thumb stopped on Mateo, the guy he'd been hooking up with.

They'd screwed quite a few times. Darrell frowned, trying to put a number on it. *Woah. A lot.* And why was he thinking of calling or texting him just for a chat? That wasn't what Darrell did. Hook-ups were just that— they weren't someone he met for lunch if he had a day off on the weekend, or went to the movies with, much less wished they were there at a work event like this. That wasn't him, just as this vague, well, *feeling*, wasn't him.

Mateo was just some guy he'd met at the gym, who he'd sounded out cagily over the weights and more openly in the locker room, and who'd jerked him off under the table in Cesar's an hour later. Oh, Darrell wasn't selfish. He'd made sure Mateo had gotten off, too, in the restroom, before they'd gone their separate ways. He'd been to the guy's apartment twice since then, and Mateo to his, neither of them spending the night, although Mateo had been amenable. Darrell hadn't.

Did he even like him? The guy was good-looking, sure, and their tastes and preferences were compatible.

Darrell liked to top and Mateo to get fucked. Hard. But Darrell certainly didn't care about him, for crap's sake. Caring was a weakness. His upbringing had told him that. His *father* had told him that.

Darrell straightened up, pushing his cell back into his pocket. "Sir," he greeted the captain, coming the other way down the corridor, flanked by detectives and civilians.

"Williams," some suit or other reminded Miller.

"Well done again." There was no handshake this time as the captain swept past.

"What's next for you after that?" asked a man with the group, making Darrell realize he was a reporter.

"The shooting range," Darrell replied. "I need to practice."

Those who'd heard chuckled, as though Darrell were making a joke, after they'd seen his performance on screen. But Darrell wasn't making any kind of quip.

Five minutes later he was there, at the range, down in the basement, a place he could ignore any and everybody else. Where he was away from the smells of coffee, cleaning chemicals and the astringent traces of pepper spray that always seemed to linger in the station and could breathe in the scents of hot metal and thick oil.

Down here, the focus was on the Smith & Wesson 40 in his hand and the target up ahead, and the three Ss that were important in life — stance, speed and spread. Here there was no room for softness or needs or wishes, and no space at all for relationships. Ear protectors muting his hearing, Darrell let a sense of calm wash over him as he steadied his breathing in the cool, climate-controlled air and squeezed the trigger to take a shot.

Chapter Three

Arriving at work the next morning, Aldric ran a hand down the front of his white button-up. He had tried to get the wrinkles out of it the night before by hanging it in the bathroom when he'd taken a hot shower, but it hadn't worked as well as he'd hoped.

His jeans were faded, although not holey, like most of his other pairs. Elliot had told him jeans were fine, but Aldric planned on buying something nicer — khakis at the very least — as soon as he could. Elliot was a classy man, and Aldric didn't want to bring any tinge of the poverty he felt emanating from him to Elliot's shop.

Poverty was the dirty secret no one ever wanted to talk about or acknowledge. It angered Aldric, but there was little he could do to change the world.

As he entered the shop, breathing deep of the wood and lacquer scents, Aldric noticed the *Help Wanted* sign was still up. He made a mental note to ask Elliot about taking it down after Elliot finished speaking with the customer he was with. He waved at Elliot, who smiled back at him, then walked behind the counter and retrieved the inventory book. Elliot had told him to study it every chance he got, and since Aldric didn't know what else he should be doing, now seemed a good time to start learning about the antiques. He polished his glasses on a tissue and got to work.

He had made it to the third page when the bells on the door chimed and an older, brown-haired man entered the shop. Elliot was still with the customer. Aldric set the inventory book down and tried to smile. "Welcome to Intrinsic Value, sir. How can I help you today?"

The man glanced from him to Elliot and back to Aldric. He tugged at the left cuff of his dark gray suit jacket. "Ah, yes. My name is Jonas Abrams. I wanted to inquire as to the nature of the position available. I have several years' experience in antiquities and a university degree that would be an asset as well."

Aldric's heart fluttered and, for a moment, he feared he'd pass out. This thick-set man, with his tortoise-shell glasses and short, close-cut mustache and beard, looked like the kind of person Elliot should have working at Intrinsic Value. He belonged there, unlike Aldric.

"Uh—" Aldric knew his face was red, a hot blush stealing over him. This would be the end of the dream job. At least he hadn't planned beyond buying new pants and paying the bills, so he wouldn't be as devastated to lose this job as he'd have been if he'd worked there longer.

"Excuse me a moment, Mr. Tibbers. I'll be right back," Elliot said before approaching not Jonas Abrams, but Aldric.

Elliot cupped Aldric's shoulder and gave it a squeeze. "Glad you made it in, Aldric. I knew I chose well."

Aldric wanted to ask if that meant he still had his job. Instead, he tried to have some faith that things might not be so serious for him. Elliot wasn't acting like he was about to fire him. "Thank you."

Elliot patted his shoulder, then faced Jonas Abrams. "I'm Elliot Douglas, the owner of Intrinsic Value. Elliot, please. And I am sorry, Mr. Abrams, but I've hired this talented young man, Aldric. I meant to take the sign down yesterday. My apologies for this inconvenience."

Mr. Abrams didn't seem to be dejected. He raised a briefcase Aldric hadn't noticed him holding. "Undoubtedly a wise decision. Aldric—may I call you by your given name?"

Aldric frowned and nodded. No one had bothered to ask his permission to say his name before. "Yes, sir."

"Oh." Mr. Abrams lowered the briefcase. "No need for that. I'm Jonas. And I would like to leave my resume with you, Elliot, if I may? I understand you've filled the position, but perhaps you might be amenable to a curator as an independent contractor? I have quite a few connections that could benefit you. If not, that is, of course, fine as well." Jonas set the briefcase on the counter and opened it.

"I'll look over your resume and take your offer into consideration. We might be able to come up with something for you here." Elliot took the resume, accepted Jonas' thanks, then waited until Jonas left the store before handing the resume to Aldric. "Put that on my desk, would you, please?"

"Yes, sir." Aldric took the resume. The paper it was printed on was thick and smooth—no doubt some expensive stuff, not the cheap packages of printer paper Aldric had bought before.

Elliot cleared his throat, and Aldric looked at him. "Sir?"

"As I just told that young man, call me Elliot, please," Elliot said, his mouth curving in the hint of a smile. "You have this job, Aldric. I'm not taking it away from you. Do you believe me?"

Aldric hated that his skittishness was so obvious. "Yes, si-er, Elliot. Thank you." He told himself to stop there, but he couldn't. "It's just that Jonas…well, he has a lot of experience and knows about this stuff already."

Elliot shrugged. "That doesn't mean you aren't an asset to this business. I'll look at his resume, and if it's impressive enough, perhaps I'll see about bringing him on part-time or exploring the options he mentioned. Whatever I decide will not result in you losing your position or hours. Do you believe me?"

Why Elliot seemed to care what Aldric believed was beyond him. Aldric didn't get creepy daddy vibes off Elliot—he just came across as a decent human being who cared about others.

"Yes, I do." Aldric exhaled a shaky breath and realized that he meant it. "Thank you. I'll be right back."

As he made his way along the narrow aisle between the table displays, wood cabinets and hand-carved dressers to Elliot's office, it took all Aldric's willpower not to read Jonas' resume. He set the paper on the desk and strode back behind the counter. Every step he'd taken had given him more confidence that he'd be able to keep this job. For whatever reason, Elliot had hired him, and Aldric would work hard to prove that Elliot hadn't made a mistake.

* * * *

Aldric had been worried when Elliot had decided to hire Jonas, but a week into working together, he had to admit that the other member of their small staff wasn't a threat to him. Once Aldric had made up his mind to let his defenses down so he could learn from Jonas, it was almost easy to let go of the worry he'd had over being fired.

Even though Aldric had only been at Intrinsic Value for a week and a half, he had a lot of the stock memorized. He was learning much faster than he'd thought he'd be capable of doing. Pride swelled in him every time Elliot asked him about some of the merchandise and he was able to answer correctly.

Jonas was a nice guy, too. He never talked down to Aldric or tried to make him feel like he was stupid for not knowing as much as Jonas or Elliot did about the antiques or what was antique and what was vintage or even retro—and what those terms meant. Jonas was employed part-time in the shop and would do contract work as well, seeking out treasures for the shop at some point in the future. He hadn't worked in a store before, and Aldric thought he'd mentioned something about teaching, or a classroom, but Jonas had changed the subject. He looked like a professor, Aldric thought.

"Aldric, the shipment has arrived! Do you want to come help me with it, and see what we've got?" Elliot tipped his chin toward Jonas, who'd just entered the shop. "Jonas can handle the front for a while."

"Yes, thanks!" A small leap of excitement shot through Aldric. He wanted to learn how to do everything related to Intrinsic Value. It wasn't only for himself. He wanted to make Elliot proud of him. Jonas, too, though it hadn't been Jonas who'd taken a chance on him.

For the first time in possibly ever, Aldric was beginning to feel like he wasn't stupid and resigned to a life of barely getting by, working shitty jobs. If he continued working for Elliot, he might even consider going to college and getting some kind of degree that would help him in the business of antiquities. That was a possibility to examine at a later time. He'd been surprised to discover a love for old things, even ones that weren't antiques. He was learning to view life, and items in it, with a different perspective.

In the stock room, Elliot removed his suit jacket. The silver vest he wore over his pale blue shirt emphasized his chest build. Aldric wondered if he'd look as neat if he dressed like Elliot. He almost felt as excited as Elliot appeared to be at the arrival of the blind shipment.

"Blind means you bought it without inspecting it, doesn't it?" Aldric hoped he'd remembered that right.

Elliot grinned and placed one hand on the biggest box on the floor. "Indeed it does. From the Buckman estate. While I wouldn't stand a chance of buying any of the deceased's priceless or luxury items, his widow wished to sell off the contents of her late husband's study. She wasn't interested in getting an appraisal to see if there was anything of real value, merely wanted everything gone. Not a wise decision on her part, and not on mine either, to purchase items unseen, but sometimes it's just...a feeling. And fun! I didn't spend a lot, either. No more than I could afford to lose. The same rule as one should follow in a casino."

Aldric couldn't imagine being able to afford to lose *any* money. He'd gotten paid on Friday, four days ago. That check, along with the one he'd get in three more days, would cover his rent and utilities. The few groceries he'd bought would have to last him, but after his second check, he figured he should be able to start saving money and buying a little more, maybe even some new clothes, although nothing as extravagant as the suits Elliot wore.

"Aldric? You drifted away on me." Elliot nudged his arm. "Did you eat breakfast?"

Aldric gave a half-nod. "Yeah, uh, yes, I had something." Tea and crackers, but it was food. "Sorry, I was thinking about antiques." He glanced up at Elliot.

Elliot studied him for a moment, then grunted. "You have a knack for antiquities, and a sharp mind like yours will be an asset to this shop. But you need to keep that brain fueled. Grab the box opener off the desk while I get a lunch sent over for all of us."

One thing Aldric had learned in his short time there was not to argue with Elliot over food. He didn't know if Elliot had, at some point in his life, been as poor and hungry as Aldric had been off and on for the past few years, although it seemed unlikely, but something must have happened to make Elliot so focused on providing for himself and his employees.

Aldric gave his glasses a quick clean then picked up the boxcutter and carefully pushed the blade out enough to cut through tape. He took his time opening the box, not wanting to risk damaging anything inside. He was working on the third and final box when Elliot returned.

"You didn't open the boxes?" Elliot sounded surprised.

Aldric finished cutting the tape and stood up. He put the blade back in the cutter and set it on the desk. "No. You ordered this stuff, so you should get to see what you got."

"Like opening gifts?" Elliot pointed to the first box. "Where's the fun in that? Go ahead and start on that one."

It *was* like opening gifts, something Aldric had little experience in. He couldn't help but smile as he parted the box top and removed the packing paper that was sticking out. The first item was a set of wooden bowls, their different sizes reminding Aldric of Russian dolls, because they all nestled into the biggest one, making them appear to be just one bowl. Their light color made him suspect they were pine. They felt very smooth and appeared to be newer than an antique would have been. He held the smallest one up and offered it to Elliot.

"What do you think of the set?" Elliot asked, taking the bowl and setting it on the desk.

Aldric had already reached for the second item but paused to answer Elliot. "They're not old. No scratches, and the wood's very thin. I thought it might be pine, but I don't know. They don't weigh much. They're not antiques." No way were the bowls over a hundred years old.

"Very good," Elliot praised. "It is a cheap faux-wood bowl. We won't put that stack on our shelves. You are welcome to take them home and use them. Otherwise, I'll throw them out."

"I'll take them. Throwing them away seems wasteful." Aldric flinched. "I didn't mean that as an insult."

"And I didn't take it as one. There is nothing at all wrong with being frugal. If you can use any of the items in this shipment that aren't going to be sold here, of course I want you to take them."

Aldric was going to ask if Jonas would want anything, but the feel of cool, inlaid metal under his fingertips distracted him. *A finger trap!* He'd only ever seen or heard of ones made of thin wood or paper, but this ornate one was something else. Working at Intrinsic Value was an adventure, and Aldric lost himself in discovering new-to-him things from the blind sale. He almost hated to stop for lunch, but the scent of hot food from the brasserie opposite was too enticing to resist.

It surprised him how quickly his days passed at work. Before he knew it, Elliot was putting the *Closed* sign up, and Jonas had left.

"I'd say we did a good day's work." Elliot patted his vest pocket, where he carried his grandfather's pocket watch.

Aldric had asked him about it when he'd seen the golden watch the first time, and Elliot had explained that it had belonged to his grandpapa. There were no such things for Aldric to inherit—not that he knew of, anyway. He was a little more envious of the connection Elliot must have had with his grandpa than he coveted the watch. It just made Aldric see how much his own familial ties were lacking.

"You're off tomorrow, but if you'd like to come in for some overtime, you can make up the stock cards on the items we received today," Elliot offered. The shipment had contained a few antiques amid the newer items.

Aldric had wondered what he'd do with his time tomorrow, and he was pleased to be given the opportunity to work. "I'll be here when you open. Thank you, Elliot."

"No problem. You're a great help, Aldric. Are you sure you don't want me to give you a ride home?" Elliot took his suit jacket off the coat rack. "It's not a problem at all, and it'd be easier than you having to carry that box onto the bus."

"No thanks. I appreciate the offer, though." Aldric didn't want Elliot or Jonas to see the decrepit garage apartment he lived in. "I'll be fine. I can lock up here, if you want? I still have to tape the box shut, and I want to dust that back shelf we didn't get to today."

Elliot frowned as he put his suit jacket on. "I wish you'd let me take you home, but I won't nag again. The back shelf can wait unless you're just set on doing it."

"My lunch break was a little over what it should have been. No way could I resist the gelato Jonas brought us." Aldric hadn't had anything so decadent in a long time. "Go on. I've got this."

Elliot had given him a set of keys to the shop his first day there. That level of trust had hit Aldric square in the chest.

Elliot paused by the counter, where Aldric was wiping down the register. "If you're not comfortable closing alone, I can hang around."

"I'm good," Aldric assured him while taking care of a persistent smudge.

"Okay. See you in the morning, then." Elliot tapped the counter, then headed out the back. "I'll lock the door behind me."

"Thanks." Aldric hummed as he finished with the register. It was his first time closing up, and he was both awed and excited. He almost felt like he was in a sacred place. To him, it was. The shop and those who worked with him were opening Aldric's eyes to new possibilities.

He hadn't realized he'd been living in a depressed state for years, and though he wasn't educated in psychology, he did believe that had been the case. It'd only taken ten days of working a job where he was treated like an actual human being rather than a target for abuse to dispel the darkness that had permeated his mind for so long. Not that he was totally free of it, but the cloud had begun to lift, and he could see now that the world wasn't all bad.

Shaking his head at his thoughts, Aldric double-checked that the front door was locked and the alarm set. The blinds were secured, shielding the shop from prying eyes and any illegal temptations that might spring up. The floor shone with a golden gleam and the wooden floors were polished to perfection. Aldric wanted to have a home with real wooden floors someday, and lots of windows.

"And space inside and out..." Aldric turned off the main lights, leaving only the security ones on. He traipsed to the office and picked up the repurposed box from the Buckman sale that contained his goodies, his favorite being the colorful teacups and saucers. Elliot had explained they were a play on words, as the term *harlequin set* meant an unmatched set of objects with a theme, so making cups with repeating patterns of contrasting diamonds, and saucers with patterns of elongated squares, no two colors the same, was a silly, subtle joke. All the items from the sale had been equally as light-hearted.

The box was bulky, but not heavy. Aldric was tempted to open it and make sure he'd packed everything well. *No.* He'd used plenty of padding, so his anxiety was not going to get the best of him here. Though it almost felt painful to do so, Aldric refused to cut the tape and double-check.

He set the box on the desk long enough to fetch his keys from his pocket, then lifted the box up and walked to the back door. The *Exit* sign glowed in the dim lighting, and for some reason, Aldric shivered. He'd heard the saying 'someone must be stepping on your grave' for such instances. He doubted that was the case, yet he couldn't shake the discomfort that came over him.

He had to put the box down again to unlock the door, prop it open with one foot, pick up his treasures again and exit. He placed the box on the ground and turned to lock the door behind him.

The blow stunned him. One second he was reaching for the box, the next, pain exploded at the back of his head. Bright starbursts bloomed in his vision—then total darkness.

Chapter Four

The San Antonio Riverwalk buzzed as it usually did, but the people strolling the narrow pedestrian walkway or clustering under the colorful café umbrellas barely registered with Darrell. He usually liked to watch the boats on the water, but today he was trying to work out what this summons could be to do with. He wasn't even sure who'd issued it. It had come from his father to the family group text, as did the usual monthly get-togethers — although this wasn't one of them — but someone else could have wanted them all to meet up.

There was no family birthday on the horizon. Maybe his elder brother, Travis, had gotten some promotion or other? Or his younger brother Ryan had aced basic training at Randolph and won some award or medal? Darrell snorted. Yeah, they'd be more likely to turn out for that sort of occasion than they would for his commendation at the station. Well, he'd only been congratulated by a captain. And the SAPD wasn't military.

"You could have joined the military police!" He heard that in three voices, because his brothers copied their father in saying it to him. Only, Darrell didn't want to be a provost, policing the armed forces. He wanted to ensure the safety of citizens, in San Antonio or wherever else he might possibly transfer to one day.

He crossed the bridge over to the stretch of more individual buildings. Brick's Tavern was the tallest of the short row, although that wasn't saying much, and seemed the most solid, at least to Darrell. Tourism sites and pages tended to describe it as traditional and unchanging, although there was nothing rundown or dingy about it.

Darrell took a deep breath and squared his shoulders, heading inside the tavern's long room. He waved a hand at any bartender or server behind or around the bar running the length of one side, even though the one he really knew, Zé, he couldn't see. A dark-haired girl waved back and twisted to call behind her, into the kitchen.

Late-afternoon sunlight glinted off the shelves of alcohol bottles and the upside-down stem glasses behind the bar and made the brass footrail gleam. The sights were as familiar to Darrell as the aroma of spicy-smoky grilling meat and salty-sharp melting cheese that filled every corner of the room and clung to clothes. He waited a second and, sure enough, clatters and thuds rang out from the ping-pong and air hockey tables in the recessed alcove at the back.

Enough nostalgia. Darrell ran up the old but well-maintained spiral steps, feeling their thump and give, to the second floor where Jack 'Chief' Williams, his father, preferred to sit.

The round table at the end of the balcony, where the big windows opened to the outside, was full of his family. He was last to arrive. He took a moment to observe the table's occupants. The three guys were dressed in 5.11 pants and had Oakley sunglasses slotted into the vee of their rolled-sleeve outdoor button-up shirts in the approved 'casual tactical' style of the special forces, for all Ryan was still in training. Darrel compared it to his own clothes. In uniform, he'd stand out more than he did already.

Darrell looked beyond the surface image, trying to gauge the mood, the reason why they were all there, and thought he'd figured it out from the way Ryan's girlfriend, Leah, had her chair so close to Ryan's that she was almost sitting in his lap.

She was the first to spot him, probably because she'd been looking out for him. "Darrell!" she squealed, making Travis' wife, Ashley, wince. Leah would have to learn to moderate her tone in the Williams family. Ashley had. "Guess what?"

A diamond ring winked on the appropriate finger of the hand she had around Ryan's arm, but Darrell didn't need the clue. "Congratulations!" he said, slapping Ryan's shoulder and bending low to kiss Leah on the cheek. "About time."

That was appropriate, wasn't it? Leah didn't seem to think so, if the speech she launched into about waiting until Ryan was almost through with basic and they knew what he'd be doing, and she was secure in the office of the company she worked in, was a clue.

He nodded in the right places, made the correct "uh-huh" noises and greeted his father. Jack stood and gripped his upper arms while looking him up and down, his version of a hug. "Let's hope so, Lea-Lea!" he said over his shoulder to Leah.

"Huh?" Darrell raised an eyebrow. He'd missed a bit.

"Your turn next," Ryan repeated his fiancée's words.

"Oh. Yeah."

"Yeah?" Travis took the ball from his brother, casting him a glance. "Got something to tell us, bro?"

Darrell wished he could. He would have loved to be able to, but the words needed to say it didn't exist in the Williams family. He gave a meaningless shrug. "So when's the wedding?"

"I just finished telling you!" Leah cried, her pitch shrill.

Jack swiveled his head in her direction and raised a finger in front of his face, as if he were going to bring it to his lips, in a gesture for silence. He didn't have to. The signal was enough. Leah reddened a little, and when she started to repeat what she'd said, both her volume and tone were lower.

Travis started in with his doings at the same time, Ryan asking questions and exclaiming over the answers, meaning Darrell still couldn't hear the wedding plans. "I got a commendation," he said, just to see if anyone responded. "For my work on a case. There's talk of me moving up to sergeant." Well, Sean had joked about it. "Or moving into criminal investigation." He had thought about becoming a detective-investigator.

"Darrell."

"Chief." The response was automatic, his father's nickname ingrained. He sat straighter.

"You see Brick on your way up? He said he'd try to get in to say hi."

"No, sir." Darrell slumped.

Brick had been in the service with Chief's father and had opened this place when he'd gotten out. His son Luke was Chief's age and had taken over, making the bar into a restaurant and bigger and better. There'd been no pressure on him to lockstep his father. Darrell wondered if Leah would have preferred to celebrate her engagement someplace else, a little more romantic, perhaps, than the place her fiancé had been coming to since he was a kid and where any minute now the server would —

His brothers cheered as the brunette, Kelly, rounded the top of the stairs and deposited the plates of hot chili-salt fries, along with the place's signature homemade condiments and pickles, on the table. There was also a helping of plantain strips — for the girls, he guessed. The shrimp platter was next, the tang of the tartar sauce and the zing of the lemon as sharp as ever. *The place we've all been coming to since we were kids and where we eat the same meal too.*

"Hey, remember that time —"

"Son."

"Sorry, Chief." Travis, recounting a story with his mouth full, stopped on a dime at his father's command and covered his mouth to chew the half a plate of fries he'd just forked in, sucking in air at the chili and garlic as he always did. Slivers of green and red pepper peeked out when he'd swallowed enough to continue. "Remember when Luke got a little fancy with the menu and added shrimp toast?"

"And Darrell said he wanted to try it and you let him!" Ryan raised his fork to his father.

Darrell remembered. They'd called him *shrimp* for at least four months. "It's good to try new things," he said in self-defense.

"Luke certainly thought so, until he realized no one wanted Gulf shrimp mousse," Jack said.

Ryan snorted and half-choked. He was more like Travis than Darrell was, for all Darrell came closer in age to Travis, the eldest, with Ryan being the youngest. "Hey, we getting the empanada platter too?" Ryan asked.

"What, the steaks not enough?" asked the guy walking up to the table. "Sorry, I couldn't get out of the kitchen until now."

"Luke!" Jack, then Travis, Darrell and Ryan greeted him in order, with Ashley and Leah following suit. The engagement news was relayed, Luke congratulating the couple and whistling over the balcony for a server to send up a round of free drinks.

"You cooking?" Jack asked.

Luke shook his head. "Zé. Says he knows just how you like 'em." Luke knew, just as his father had, how regulars liked their meat. Well, their orders in general.

"Guess we'll see," Chief replied.

Luke took a quick seat. Darrell had known he would. He could even have predicted which table he'd spin it from, and where he'd place it, just as he knew which turn the conversation would take now.

"Engaged. Doesn't seem a minute since Ryan graduated from burgers to steak." Luke shook his head. "You told that lady of yours about those crazy competitions you and your brother had, seeing how much you could add to a burger? Cheese, bacon, onion rings…"

"Avocado, tomato, fried egg!" Ryan used his hands to show the height of the burger with the extras.

"So that's where you got your bad eating habits from!" Leah slapped his arm. No one spoke, but Ashley cut her eyes at Leah. "And you grew up big and strong." Leah stroked her palm over Ryan's biceps.

"And didn't Darrell work his way through one sandwich after another for, like, a whole year?" Ashley asked. "And you worked out he was going in reverse order up the list—"

"And the first one had pork butt!" Travis fed her a plantain chip.

Yeah, that had been a nickname too.

"Well, everything on the menu's good!" Luke joked, getting to his feet.

True. And Darrell could just go for a bologna sandwich now, despite the teasing. He wouldn't say no to going to play on the old skill machines down below. He'd leave the table football and ring toss to the others, his father included, like he always used to. He changed his mind when Luke, having fussed with the table and the space next to it, beckoned his son over with the portable stand to cook their steaks tableside.

"Zé." Darrell gave him a big smile, Zé shooting him a sly wink in return. Zé was gay. Darrell had seen him out with a couple of different guys over the last few years. If things were different, he'd have liked to sit down and chat with Zé over a beer. They had a lot in common and, yeah, Darrell found him sexy. He watched Zé's deft movements in slapping the tenderloin over to fry its other side in the garlic herb butter.

Travis used the noise and commotion of frying and plating as a cover to lean into Darrell and say, "Yeah, he knows his way around meat. So I heard."

"You did?" Darrell kept his eyes front. "Where d'you go to pick up that sort of gossip?"

Travis spent a few seconds working out if that was an insult. "Just to warn you." He made sure he was turned completely away from the others. "Because the way you were looking, like you were eyeing something hot and juicy...and I don't mean the steaks!" He snorted then laughed.

"What?" Ryan called over, hating to miss a joke.

"Nothing," Darrell told him. "Planning your bachelor evening." *Let that worry Travis.* His phone buzzed and he glanced at the screen. "Oh, I gotta take this. One minute."

He walked away to relative privacy to answer. "Mateo?" They never Facetimed. Had only called each other once. Their communication was the quickest of messages. "What's the matter?"

"How's it going with the family?" Mateo's tan face and bright blue eyes filled the screen.

"Huh?"

"You said you were meeting up to have an early dinner. Didn't seem too keen on it. But it's going okay?"

"I..." He'd mentioned this personal detail, when they'd met at Cesar's two nights ago, before going to Mateo's to fuck?

"Want me to drop by, really give them something to talk about?"

"Jesus, no." Darrell's horror wasn't just at the thought. It was fine for Travis and Ryan to bring home girls or bring them to Bricks' meals, but he could not imagine Chief Williams' reaction to a son of his seeing a guy.

But he wasn't. Didn't. Any guys he hooked up with were just that, fuck buddies.

"Okay. Jeez." Mateo looked a little affronted. "Wanna meet later, talk about it? Or...not talk?" he added, when Darrell's silence stretched.

"No. I don't know. I have to go. I'll text." He cut the call and eased his way out of the space behind the top of the staircase.

"Oh, hi!" Leah stood and waved at a girl who'd just reached the top of the stairs. She beckoned her and Darrell, just behind her, over. "This is Brianna from work. She has an appointment nearby, right, Bri, so she said she'd drop by and say congratulations and hi to y'all. Can you stay for a little while, Bri?"

Darrell's heart plummeted, more so when Ryan added, "Move around there. Can we get an extra chair?" with a meaningful smile at Darrell. His reaction to the new arrival screamed foreknowledge and even rehearsal.

Darrell got through it. Through Brianna being pressed to stay to eat. Through his father and Luke discussing the big football game coming up and how they'd all be going to support their old high school, and Darrell was coming of course, no argument. He could have predicted the invitation to Brianna to come along too, if not Leah's exact, heavy-handed, "Darrell, Bri's a recent transplant to the Military City and needs someone to help her experience its flavor!"

They'd reached the stage of looking at the dessert suggestions on the menu, even though they'd all go for an ice cream at The Parlor, the traditional end to a Williams meal, when Darrell's radio buzzed. He excused himself to answer and had rarely been so happy to get a call.

"Son!" Jack reproached.

"I got a couple of hours off, with time banked, but I'm on call." Darrell smiled at Bri. "Have my ice cream for me. Mint choc chip." In that, he was unchanging. God alone knew what would ever have happened if he'd tried out tutti-frutti.

On the way to where Sean was picking him up, he dropped a quick text to Mateo, saying he thought they should cool things down, give each other a rest. Mateo's call had made him realize that the other guy was assuming that their relationship was evolving beyond Darrell bending him over any available surface and fucking his brains out—and that Darrell was in danger of falling into that trap too.

Better to disarm that ticking bomb now, before it went off in his face.

Chapter Five

"Mister? Sir? Are you *dead*?"

"Oh shit, I think he is! The dude's, like, croaked, right here in front of us. I'm *freaked*, man!"

"No, look—he's breathing, see?"

"No, I don't *wanna* see. What the hell you *doing* to him?"

"I'm trying to feel a pulse in his neck, like on the cop shows. Yeah, I got one! He's okay."

"Call that okay? Jesus! I'm calling nine-one-one. Hey, maybe we'll be on the news for saving the dude!"

Aldric figured he couldn't be dead, since he was hurting so much. There was no way he could even open his mouth to tell anyone this and doubted his voice would work even if he could. He tried to open his eyes instead and groaned as pain ricocheted around his skull.

"Mister, just take it easy." Something patted his shoulder. "T's calling for help. You got a signal, T?"

Panic zipped through Aldric and he couldn't get his mind to work the way he wanted it to. He opened his eyes and yelped, then cringed at the pain he'd caused himself by being loud.

"Dude, chill. I swear we aren't gonna hurt you."

That was the voice belonging to the guy who wasn't 'T'.

Aldric blinked away the spots dancing in front of his eyes. He had trouble focusing for a few seconds. A kid who had to be in his mid-teens was leaning over him, one hand pressed to Aldric's chest. "Glasses?" Aldric gritted out.

"Oh. Hold on…here! Lucky I didn't step on 'em." The kid held them out. "Lucky as well they're not broken." When Aldric just blinked at him, he carefully placed his glasses on for him.

"You'll be okay. I'm Dave. That's T, on the phone over there." Dave tipped his head to the left and Aldric, moving slowly so as not to hurt himself more, managed to cut his gaze in that direction.

The dark-haired boy named T was talking so fast into the phone that Aldric had trouble following what he was saying. *Spanish. He's speaking Spanish.* Aldric only knew the basics of it, which explained why he was confused about what was being said.

"We should hear sirens any minute now. You remember what happened? Like, how you fell?" Dave asked, a falsely cheerful, reassuring note in his tone.

Aldric moved his gaze back to Dave. Dave also had dark hair. Other than that, Aldric didn't think the two boys looked alike. "No, but…I'm…f-fine," he forced out.

Dave rolled his eyes. "I don't think so, dude. You were out cold. We—"

"Thought I was dead," Aldric cut in. He started to sit up and immediately regretted it. "Oh, God."

"Uh, yeah, man. Stay down there. You're kinda green." Dave winced. "Listen — sirens. Told ya."

"Sirens." Aldric groaned again, thinking of the cost he could incur even if his health insurance was active. "Tell them to go back."

"No can do. You kinda made a mess of yourself when you tripped, or whatever."

"He didn't fall," T said with authority. "Look at the mess. Not him. The other mess, I mean."

Aldric winced at having been called a mess three times in a minute.

"T!" Dave's gesture at his friend seemed to be asking for politeness.

If so, it didn't work. "Shit's all over." T took a couple of steps, kicking at things.

"Careful!" the more cautious Dave urged. "That's an antiques store back there, man!"

Under other circumstances, Aldric might have smiled at that. Now, though, he doubted he could make his facial muscles obey his bidding.

"So, unless he fell and ripped open that box, then stomped on everything in it —"

"Everything?" Aldric struggled to remember what happened but couldn't. "I don't understand. I guess I dropped the box, when… No. I put it down." He thought he recalled leaving the store. "Maybe I fell on top of it?"

"What, like a few times, up and down again? And that was after a knife sticking out of your pocket ripped the cardboard open?" T said scornfully.

"*Aldric!*"

He recognized that voice before he saw Elliot running over to him, a panicked expression on his boss' face.

"Aldric, what happened? I get an alert when the alarm goes off and —" Elliot clapped a hand to his mouth, blanched and swayed.

"Shoot, help him!" Dave instructed to T, who grabbed Elliot by the biceps and encouraged him to sit, making him take a few steps first to a cleaner bit of the ground.

"Don't worry. He's okay," T said to Elliot. "Does the blood make you want to pass out? My brother's like that. He's a badass until he sees blood, then bam! He's down. Real handicap when you wanna be an MMA fighter, huh?"

"Blood?" Aldric reached for his head. That was what hurt the most.

"Maybe you hit it when you fell?" Dave suggested as Aldric's fingers encountered a wet, sticky fluid at the back of his head. He brought his hand slowly around to his face and tried to focus on the substance coating his skin.

"I bet whoever robbed him hit him first," T countered, as blunt as ever.

"*Robbed him*? What do you mean?" Elliot's voice shook and sounded weak. "Aldric, what happened? Damn, I shouldn't have left you here all by yourself. I should have insisted —"

"I'm an adult," Aldric ground out. He forced himself to leave the injury alone, wiping his hand on a paper tissue Dave held out. He brought his hand to his side, then pushed himself — slowly — into a sitting position. "This isn't your fault."

"Duh, it's the fault of whoever hit you and smashed up your stuff." Dave added an eye-roll along with his words. "Seems obvious."

54

Elliot opened his mouth but snapped it shut again when sirens blared close by. He moved over to Aldric's side, Dave and T stepping away.

Aldric expected to see EMTs rounding the corner, reassuring in their controlled haste and carrying whatever was needed to make him feel better. Instead, two police officers appeared, shoulder-to-shoulder, implacable and unreadable. One man was taller and lankier, his black hair shining even in the poor lighting, and the other was shorter and stockier looking. Both had their guns drawn. The sight of the two cops, moving as one, all practiced speed and stealth with their weapons in their hands, tested Aldric's bladder restraint. He was glad it held up. He hated guns with a passion, a leftover borderline-phobia from his first job. He'd bet anyone working in fast food who'd had an active shooter on the premises would hate guns too.

Elliot held out a hand toward the officers. "Please. None of us are the bad guy here, officers. I'm Elliot Douglas, owner of the antique store behind us. Aldric Beamer is my employee, and he's been hurt. These two young men are…well…um."

The cops looked at Dave and T. Both boys held their hands up. "We called for y'all," Dave said. "T called, and I sat with that dude—Aldric, is it? Cool name. I only touched him to check for a pulse and to put his glasses on for him." He went to lower one hand, perhaps to show the cops on his own neck where he'd rested his fingers on Aldric's, but a slight shift by both uniformed men had him raising it again.

T bobbed his head. "Yeah, I can show you the call on my phone." He still had his cell in one hand and shook it slightly in illustration.

"What were you two doing back here?" the more built cop asked of the boys.

Dave lowered his hands. Slowly. "We always cut through the alley to get to the apartments where we live in at the next block over. It's shorter than staying on the sidewalk. We're usually through here earlier, but T and I got parts in our school's play and we had our first rehearsals just this afternoon, so we were later coming this way."

"And you found this man—" This time, the wirier police officer spoke, glancing at Aldric. "Aldric Beamer?"

"Yeah, we thought he was dead at first. It was creepy!" Dave's words came out in a rush. "He was so still, and there's blood, and all that broken stuff scattered around. We didn't see anyone else."

"I need you two to remain where you are. Mr. Douglas, Mr. Beamer, can you corroborate their story?" the shorter officer asked, his voice hard.

"I was unconscious, but I came to with them trying to help me, and, er, T on the phone with emergency services." Aldric blinked as he tried to remember what had happened between that time and earlier, when he'd left the shop. "I was leaving, by the back door, then…" Then he had no idea. He'd woken up in this pain.

A noise at the mouth of the alley had him turning his head to see…and instantly regretting it. More police officers filled the space, with two EMTs right on their heels. Aldric lost track of the cops' questions. He noted there were no more drawn guns, and two officers were talking to Dave and T, while another spoke to Elliot.

One of the cops that had arrived after the first two might have been questioning Dave, but he was watching Aldric. Aldric stared back. The guy was average height, but better built than average, and had a square jaw and blunt chin. His eyes were dark, at least Aldric thought they were. He couldn't see them well in the gloom of the alley, yet he felt the man's gaze like a searchlight turned on him.

Does that guy think I'm guilty of something? That I was trying to rob Elliot's store? Or maybe that all this is a hoax? Aldric could never do anything to hurt Elliot, and the way he was feeling was no ruse. Perhaps because he was shaken up, Aldric found the courage to snap at the cop, "Why are you staring at me? Who are you?"

"I'm Officer Darrell Williams." The cop's voice was clipped, terse, maybe, but not unpleasant.

Aldric racked his brain, trying to figure out if that name should be familiar and came up empty. "So?"

Williams approached, eyes narrowed, looking every bit like the bad cop in every stereotypical good-cop, bad-cop TV show Aldric had ever watched. It irked Aldric. He'd just been attacked and was bleeding in a grimy alley, so why was this Williams guy treating him like that? "What?" Aldric spat out, in a way he never would have dreamed of doing ordinarily, and to a police officer least of all. "You got something to say, say it."

"Just, you say you were robbed, but nothing was stolen from you? You still got your wallet? It seems odd that you —"

"You can ask him questions after he's taken care of," Elliot interrupted, pushing his way past Williams as if he weren't afraid of the police at all. "Your tone is incredibly rude. Aldric's been hurt. He's the victim, not the perpetrator or one of the perpetrators. If you want to be obnoxious to him, I can make sure my lawyer handles all the questions you might have."

"Why would he need a lawyer?" Williams asked. "And I wasn't being obnoxious. I—"

Elliot growled, a sound Aldric had never heard him make before. "Oh, for the love of God! Stop harassing him. What is your problem?"

"Williams, come here," someone called. "Now."

Williams stared for another second, then turned and walked off.

"Some cops," Elliot muttered. "I can say that because I once knew a police officer—well, a detective—who was great at his job. That guy who was snapping at you, not so much."

Aldric couldn't help agreeing about the Williams part of that statement, but tried to be fair. "Maybe he's having a bad day, or...or he's the bad cop in the scenario. And it could look suspicious, me being hurt but nothing being taken."

"Or it could mean someone is out to hurt you specifically." Elliot pursed his lips. "Damn it. I should not have said that. It's possible the boys interrupted a would-be robbery."

Aldric was stuck on the first of Elliot's ideas, that someone had meant to hurt him, that he had been the goal, not his merchandise or money. *But what does that mean?*

The wave of nausea that hit him, making him twist around and vomit, might have been caused by his head injury—or the fear that Elliot was right.

Chapter Six

Spending even one night in the hospital was not going to happen. Aldric flat-out refused, despite how bad he was feeling. "I must have already racked up thousands of dollars in debt!"

Elliot frowned. "Your insurance will cover most of it. We have an excellent plan. Workman's Comp is also going to be involved since you were hurt on the job. You won't have to pay anything. You're staying until they release you, then you'll come home with me until the doctor gives you an all-clear to be by yourself."

Aldric tried not to pout. His emotions were all over the place, which wasn't usual for him. He'd been on the verge of tears more than once since coming to the hospital.

"Hmm. You don't seem too keen on that. Do you have family or friends to go stay with?" Elliot scrutinized him. "Friends other than myself you'd prefer to let assist you?"

His cheeks burning hot with embarrassment, Aldric couldn't look at Elliot. He took off his glasses and studied the new chip in the frame, courtesy of the alley's concrete. "No."

"Then you'll stay with me. I'll go to your place and grab some clothes. Is there anything specific you want me to get from your apartment?" Elliot asked.

"No." Aldric looked down at his chest. No, he didn't want Elliot, his wealthy, cultured boss, seeing the crappy place he lived in. Not that Elliot would belittle him for it, or say anything about it, probably, but he'd see it, and look at Aldric, and... Aldric gave up trying to sort through all the ways in which Elliot would react to both the decrepit studio apartment above a garage and to Aldric afterward.

"Or I can stop by Target and get you a few things on the way to my home," Elliot said after a moment. "That might be better."

Aldric would need more clothes, and toiletries, if he were staying anywhere other than his own home. He was torn between telling Elliot not to buy him anything, because he hadn't budgeted for it and couldn't afford it, and relief at knowing that if he agreed to the purchases, Elliot wouldn't see his place.

"I'll drop by Target, and you are not to worry. We'll work out a payment arrangement for anything I pick up for you, unless it's something you hate and want to return, of course." Elliot stood and stretched.

That he'd be staying at Elliot's belatedly registered with Aldric. A guest in someone's house? And him injured, probably needing care or help or... Worry bubbled up, chased by anxiety, both of them making his head throb more. He put a hand to it.

Elliot followed the movement of Aldric's hand, and his lips thinned. "I'm sorry you were hurt, Aldric. That shouldn't have happened. I'll be contacting the alarm company about installing cameras and ensuring we have the best security services available. Oh, and here comes Jonas to check on you too. I struck gold, hiring you both."

Aldric wasn't sure about that, not in regard to himself. He closed his eyes and remembered the article he'd read on self-confidence. Insulting himself wasn't going to make him smarter or more successful. He couldn't afford to go to college yet, but he *could* become a better person in many ways as long as he tried. To that end, he'd been researching some of the issues he knew he had, and he'd realized he didn't have to be unseen, someone who barely survived. He had value. For some reason, an image of that police officer flashed in his head, the man's short dark brown hair and dark eyes as clear as day. What color had they been? A kind of brown?

"Aldric?"

Aldric blinked, then blinked again as he tried to focus. Jonas was standing beside the hospital bed. A wrinkle marred his brow, making him appear older than usual.

"You drifted off." Jonas' frown deepened and he looked at Elliot.

"I imagine his injury has a lot to do with that," Elliot said.

"How do you feel?" Jonas asked.

Aldric tried to focus. "My head hurts," was the best he could manage.

Jonas sat in Elliot's chair by the bed. "Elliot told me what happened. It's very strange. I checked the shop as he asked me to. Nothing was missing from it. The police finished up there while I was doing a quick inventory. I don't know exactly what was in the box of stuff you were carrying, but none of it survived." He winced. "I don't know why someone would do that—attack you, break your things and leave."

"The guys who found me might have scared the person off," Aldric said. His head pounded and he bit back a moan.

"And on top of that, some Neanderthal of a police officer was rude to him," Elliot told Jonas.

"No!" Jonas indicated Aldric where he lay in a hospital bed, no doubt pale and pathetic-looking.

"Yes." Elliot thinned his lips. "He was a real brute."

"He…" Aldric didn't know what he was going to say. "Was probably having a bad day." He tried a shrug, or as much of one as he could manage without making his head move too much.

"I was, but that's no excuse."

Aldric jumped, then groaned. The jarring had hurt. He wasn't hallucinating, was he? That guy, that cop—all crew cut and piercing gaze—from the alley was here, in the hospital room, speaking to him. He snuck glances at Elliot and Jonas to check if they saw and heard him too.

"Officer?" Elliot, his normally placid face taking on some of the anger it had at the scene of the crime, got between the man and Aldric. Jonas sprang to his feet and joined the human barrier too. "Why are you here? Do you have more questions for Aldric? Because if so, what I said earlier stands—you should ask them through my lawyer, who—"

"No." The cop's upraised hand cut Elliot off. "I…"

I just said the first thing that came into my head in that alley, when he caught me staring. Yeah, that should go down great. Darrell pulled his gaze from the pale, bruised figure in the bed and switched it to Elliot. "I came to apologize." He included Aldric as he continued, "I was curt. Rude."

"You were indeed." Elliot Douglas pursed his lips.

"*Green!*"

"Excuse me?" Darrell said to Aldric, who'd uttered the word, in a tone of discovery. "What—"

"Dark green." Aldric colored, and it made his hospital-pale complexion look sallow. "Nothing. I'm concussed. But, you, earlier…it's okay."

"It's not." Darrell clasped his arms behind his back, his feet shoulder-width apart. "I'm here to apologize."

"You've done enough, from the sound of it." The other man by Aldric's bed, who Darrell presumed was a co-worker, joined the chorus.

"Is there a problem here?" The doctor Darrell had seen outside entered, looking from one person to another. He half-turned to the nurse with him, raising his eyebrows in what Darrell judged to be a pre-established signal that she could alert security.

"No, sir." Darrell snapped open his wallet and presented his SAPD badge.

The doctor nodded to the nurse, who pushed the dispensing trolley over to the bed and passed Aldric a small medical cup and a larger cup of water to swallow down the meds that the plastic beaker contained.

"This is the officer who was called to the scene of the attack," Mr. Douglas explained.

Attack. That word hurt. Aldric reacted to it, and Darrell flinched for him. Aldric was bruised, yes, but still, well—*beautiful*, was the adjective pushing its way to the forefront of Darrell's mind, ambushing him with its softness and gentleness.

Aldric hunched into himself, and Darrell wanted nothing more right then than to make him uncurl. *To bloom.* He pulled himself together and addressed the doctor. "Can Mr. Beamer leave? I'd like to offer him a ride home." *To make up for my behavior earlier*, he didn't add, because he wasn't sure that was the entire reason.

The doctor straightened with a grunt from where he'd been bending down to Aldric and shining a pen light in his eyes. "He can, yes. He has mild concussion following his loss of consciousness of less than thirty minutes, but he's alert and his pain is managed." He gave one of those fleeting medical smiles that doctors were too busy to let settle, then finished scribbling on Aldric's chart. "But he shouldn't stay alone, of course."

"I'll stay with him." Darrell jutted out his chin at Aldric's boss and co-worker, his watchdogs, when protests sprang to their lips.

Aldric pushed off his hospital sheet, then swung his feet to the floor. "That would be fine." He swayed a little, surprise on his face that Darrell thought was maybe due to what he'd just said, as though he hadn't known he was going to say that, or why he had. He stood straight and added, "Thank you."

Darrell smiled. That was good enough for him.

* * * *

He wished he had more clothes for Aldric to wear. His were dirty and his shirt had blood down the back of the collar. Still, Aldric had accepted his jacket to wear over it. Darrell snuck looks at him where he was sitting next to Darrell in the passenger seat of Darrell's pickup, and more than once his gaze snagged with Aldric's, because Aldric was doing the same to him.

"So—"

"Don't ask me anything about what happened. I can't remember more than I said. I didn't see anything before or when I was out. Well, I wouldn't." Aldric's brow creased.

"I wasn't. I was going to say I'm rarely in this area. It's one of the calmer ones." Darrell tilted his head at the streets they were driving along. Did Aldric usually babble on like that? It was— Again, soft adjectives like *sweet* and *endearing* surprised him. Aldric was looking better, too. While still tight with tension, he had more color, and the pain meds must have been kicking in.

"It's an old neighborhood. And an old apartment. Just along here." Aldric's voice had dropped to a mutter as they approached a small square building set back a little from the bigger house to one side of it.

Darrell cleared his throat. "It's—"

"Decrepit. Oh, a charming garage conversion into a bijou vintage town home, I'm supposed to say. Maybe it even was, back in the day."

"Would you stop interrupting me and saying what you think I'm thinking?" It wasn't the meds that were loosening Aldric's tongue, Darrell would have bet. He pulled up near the building then walked behind Aldric, not helping him but near enough to, while he headed up the steps to the unit. Darrell's eyes were drawn to Aldric's bubble butt. It was as cute as his rambling. The guy seemed timid, yet Darrell remembered how he'd challenged him, back in the alley. *And look at me, checking out a guy with a head injury, who's just out of hospital. Je-sus.*

Aldric hesitated, his key in hand, and Darrell eased forward. "Here. Let me." The key stuck and needed forcing, as did the door, but he got it open and stood back for Aldric to enter.

"This is the living area," Aldric announced, unnecessarily, in the tiny hall space just inside. He spoke to the floor. "And there's the kitchenette and dinette. Lots of ettes. Bathroom. Bedroom, with patioette. If that's a word. I grew up in this area and when my parents sold up and moved — they couldn't wait any longer and it wasn't fair to make them — this came up."

He half-twisted and gestured on the word *this* and because Darrell was so close, Aldric's hand landed on his chest. Aldric looked startled, more so when Darrell trapped it with his. Aldric looked from their hands to Darrell's face. He opened and closed his mouth a few times, but Darrell got in first, fascinated by this man.

"What's green?"

"Your eyes." Aldric tried to clear his throat and gave up. "I wondered. I didn't see the color clearly."

Darrell grinned, enjoying this. "See 'em now?"

Aldric nodded.

"You keep telling me what I'm thinking — and getting it wrong — so what are they saying?" he asked.

Aldric dipped his head, but Darrell's hand under his chin, where his fingers stroked the soft skin they found, stopped him. Instead Aldric raised his eyes to Darrell's face.

"Can't you guess? That I want you?" Darrell asked.

Darrell's words thrilled Aldric. They shot through him like a bolt of lightning, sizzling a path. Answers rumbled together in his brain like gumballs fighting to get down a chute, but what came out was, "I want you too." Before his brain could catch up with his mouth, could take back those words, he'd moved, and so had Darrell—to grab his hips and kiss him.

His brain tried to second-guess, but Aldric told it to shut the hell up and opened his mouth under the pressure of Darrell's lips against his, then gasped as Darrell swept his tongue in—tasting, and *learning*, was the only description Aldric could supply, when his brain was stuck on the word *swept. Swept in and swept me away.* Wanting to escape his own thoughts, he pressed close. Tight. And didn't flinch when Darrell's hand moved from his side to his lower back, and his ass. It squeezed and caressed, and as if there were a direct connection, Aldric's cock thickened in his pants, the swiftness of his reaction shocking him.

Darrell moved so there was no gap between them, only contact, then hummed low in his chest. It vibrated along every nerve ending in Aldric's body and gathered in his balls. As if Darrell knew, he shifted to put a little distance between them, enough to get his hand to Aldric's crotch and duplicate the stroking he was doing to Aldric's ass on his cock. Aldric's dick grew more erect still, as if wanting to push into Darrell's fingers.

No. Too much, too soon, after too long. After never. Aldric's brain was trying, but all his blood was pooling lower, while Darrell caressed him. Aldric tore his mouth from Darrell's and twisted his body away too, but too late. His arousal thundered, ripped from him, and he came in his pants. A dismayed, disbelieving sound forced itself from his lungs and he hunched over.

"Hey."

He wasn't going to look up. Ever.

"It's okay. Been a while?"

He wasn't speaking again, either. Ever.

"We can move this to the bedroom and—"

"I don't— I mean I haven't. Not like this." Okay, so he *was* speaking, even if it made no sense. He risked a tiny peek up. *So I'm looking again too.* "Hook-ups. Just meet and well, get down to it. I don't know how to." He forced himself to straighten up and dragged his gaze along Darrell's body to his chest. "Let me go clean up. Then I'll make some tea, and we can talk. You're staying anyway, right? We can get to know each other a bit." He finally managed to look Darrell in the eye.

Darrell was frozen, like a deer in the headlights. He heaved in a ragged breath, then backed away, giving tiny shakes of his head. He clapped a hand to his chest as light played over it. Actual headlights, followed by the sharp *pah-pah-pah* blast of the horn Selena always gave.

"Huh? That's my cousin." Aldric didn't understand why she'd be here at the best of times, let alone this time of night. "Oh, I had her down as next-of-kin. The hospital must have called her!"

Darrell had reached the door by now and opened it behind him. "So she'll stay with you? Aldric…I-I don't do talk and getting-to-know. Sorry."

And he was gone, leaving Aldric alone, confused and with his pants full of cooling cum.

Chapter Seven

Sean shot Darrell a look. "You wanna drive? Is that the reason for all the clenching your fists and sighing?"

"What? Oh, no." Darrell stretched out his fingers and made an effort to focus on the here and now.

"I know people think I got a lead foot." Sean turned the patrol car onto one of The Dominion's smaller avenues. "My ma gets really Catholic in the car with me, clutching her crucifix and crossing herself."

"You drive fine. Just thinking. Nice houses."

They should be. The neighborhood was the most affluent in the San Antonio area. It was hard to see most of the houses, with them being set far back from the road and their grounds screened by mature trees.

Mature. Funny, he'd just been brooding again on what an *im*mature jerk he'd been to Aldric. It had been three days ago now and still Darrel's face heated when he thought about how he'd left the guy. How he'd *behaved* toward the guy, and not just in walking out on him like that.

He'd been snappy with him when they'd met. What had Aldric's boss called him, a Neanderthal? *About right.* Then taking advantage of a victim of an assault. Aldric had been whacked out on pain pills, for fuck's sake, and yet Darrell had moved in on him.

He moved on me back, a small voice in his head argued. It replayed images of Aldric's lips parting and his mouth opening for Darrell's tongue. Of his dick pushing into Darrell's hand. His dick that had shot its load within minutes because Aldric wasn't used to —

The thought that it could have been the guy's first time had Darrell turning to stone, his lungs trying to quit working on him.

He forced himself to breathe, then to talk. "So, you looking for something like this, when you and Daniela move in together?" He nodded at the grounds Sean was turning the police vehicle into.

"*She* would if she could, yeah. This looks like a resort, man!"

It did. Like some place for a beyond-his-paygrade all-inclusive vacation. Sean slowed for the crime scene techs in their van behind them to catch up, then continued past the massive house and round to the casita, a smaller-scale version near the pool. "We couldn't even afford this," Sean commented.

A woman was waiting outside the vandalized casita, and Sean went to greet her then drew her away to let forensics get to work. Darrell thought he'd be better employed looking over the scene before he joined his partner and the vic. The damage was minimal. A few windows all in a line had been smashed, as though someone had run past them and hit one after the other, but more interesting was the spray-painted graffiti.

"D'you mind?" The plastic-suited guy elbowed him roughly out of the way to take pictures.

"What's put a bug up your ass?" Darrell asked, standing his ground.

"Let's just say I *really* don't like being pulled off a more serious, more urgent case for this, just so Miller can say his most experienced crime scene team is on it. Any science technician with field training could work this SOC." The guy snapped pictures and spared Darrell a glance. "You don't look like the station's most senior patrol officer, though."

"The most charming." Darrell indicated Sean, who was either consoling or calming down the vic. At least that raised a smile from the technician. Darrell took a few pictures himself on his phone then headed over to Sean and the owner of the house, trying to interpret Sean's expression.

"My partner, Officer Darrell Williams." Sean introduced him to the mid-thirties, auburn-haired woman clutching a linen handkerchief. "Mrs. Randa Buckman, Buck Buckman's widow."

"I'm very sorry for your loss." Darrell tried to recall exactly when her husband had died. Not quite a week ago, he thought, recalling the news stories about the real estate billionaire. "And I'm sorry this has happened to you. But we'll do our best to catch whoever's responsible, of course."

"Mrs. Buckman thinks she knows who did it." Sean's voice sounded like he was swallowing something.

"Oh?" Darrell flipped open his notebook. Someone or something connected to her late husband, he'd bet. A business rival? Jim 'Buck' Buckman had been one of the richest men in the county, making a fortune in real estate. Not just industrial parks for science and IT companies – his company had been one of the groups that had developed the Cultural Corridor, part of the Riverwalk.

Darrell did the math on this woman's age compared to Buck's and came up with *second* or *third*. As in wife. Meaning predecessors. Randa, left all this by Buck's death, could have her own rivals too. "Who do you think's responsible, ma'am?"

"My husband!" Randa buried her face in the handkerchief she'd been twisting in her hands. Darrell looked at Sean, and Sean looked back. "My late husband, I mean. Buck. Did you read the message?"

"It said 'I want my puzzles', right?" It had puzzled *him*, and Sean shrugged in incomprehension too.

"Exactly." Randa nodded at Darrell. "He wants to be reunited with his puzzles."

"His…?"

"That's his writing, on the wall there!" Randa's voice rose, but she fanned her face and got herself calm. "It's my fault. I couldn't bear to walk into his study and see all that stuff he collected. Oh, not the artwork and priceless stuff for his collections. That's displayed throughout the house. I mean the little curios and games he had on the tables in his room. He spent so much time tracking bits and pieces down and buying them, and so much time with them when he'd gotten them. I had to get rid of it, just sell it all as a job lot. Seeing it without him, I mean."

"Which puzzles in particular?" Darrell was making a few notes.

"Boxes. Those little Oriental ones you can't open." Randa held her hands a few inches apart in demonstration. "He loved playing with them, trying to get them to give up their secrets, as he called it. He got off on the challenge. Soon as he solved one, he moved to the next. They took up half his desk. He liked all the curiosities he got, but he adored those little wooden Japanese boxes. Any visitors we had, he'd see if they could work out the secret of his latest one, or his favorite one. And I sold them!"

It was awkward, watching her sob, head bent and the handkerchief covering her face. An assistant came up with a glass of water and put it into her hand. Randa swallowed some, then handed it back and raised her head. "I joked that he wanted to be buried with them, that he loved those stupid mosaic wood boxes, and he agreed. I didn't know he meant it."

"Well, how could you have?" Sean kept his voice neutral. Darrell could hear already how he'd be recounting this later, laughing it up about how they didn't need crime scene techs from the lab to catch a criminal, but a priest from the church to lay a ghost to rest.

"What have I done?" Randa turned from one to another. "What if he can't cross over to be at peace, with his spirit disturbed, and that's why he's wandering here, doing this? What's going to happen next?" She scrunched the handkerchief and pressed it to her mouth, her hand shaking.

"Let's not borrow trouble, ma'am. I have a few questions, if that's okay?" When Randa nodded, Darrell took her through the when and how of the vandalism.

"No, the security cameras don't cover that entrance to the casita," she told him in answer to a question. "I'll have some installed there now, though."

And no one in the main house had heard anything. Interviewing the two members of staff who lived in had confirmed that.

"We taking a look around the house?" Darrell asked Sean, who shook his head.

"Negative."

Decided higher up. Darrell got it. And yeah, with forensics not finding obvious footprints or traces of an intruder anywhere on the grounds, there seemed little point. Randa thought so too. There'd been no B&E, no robbery. No sign at all that anyone had been there…except for Buck, whose handwriting Randa was sure the graffiti was in, telling them this three times in total.

"Why don't they have security cameras on this entrance or on this section of the pool house?" he wondered.

Sean hid a laugh. Amusement at crime scenes was a no-no. "It's real easy to see you don't have a *chica*. If you did, you'd catch at least some of these Rich Housewives of Where The Fuck Ever programs."

"And?"

"And if you did, you'd know the pool house is where the rich go for their quick fucks with their side pieces when their other half's out."

"But which other half?" A marriage was two people. Either Buck or Randa could have made use of the casita. "But would that have anything to do with the vandalism?"

"What you thinking? One of the help's trying to mess with her?" Sean asked.

"Could be." The vandalism, although costly, felt half-assed to Darrell. "But whatever, she seems keen on getting those boxes, the puzzles, back. I'm wondering... She said they were Japanese, right?" He reread his notes. "What if they, or one or more, were valuable? Like, jade or ivory or something? Some priceless antique she sold cheap and now wants back?"

It clicked then. Hit him, rather, making him want to stagger, like Aldric had done. "Fuck, Sean, she sold them to Intrinsic Value! That antique store where the employee got hit from behind when he was leaving with a box of stuff from—"

"The estate sale!" Sean was right there with him. "But the guy, and the boss, said the box was full of worthless stuff, cheap crap that they wouldn't sell in the store, right?"

"They *said*, yeah, but..." Darrell let his shrug say neither he nor Sean were experts in appraising antiques. He flipped through his notebook. "Elliot Douglas gave Aldric Beamer some valueless items."

He liked saying Aldric's full name and was glad to have an excuse to think about Aldric. His tangle of dark hair, his dark brown eyes peeping shyly at the world from behind his round glasses, then flashing with determination. He was contradictory. *Intriguing.* Darrell had been fascinated from that first glimpse.

That interest had propelled him to the hospital, where he'd acted on impulse in offering Darrell a ride home. *And offered to stay with him, hoping for a different kind of ride.* The little voice, half devil on his shoulder, half conscience, was back. *Not like he wasn't willing.* The idea of being the first to give the timid yet hot Aldric his first ass-fuck had Darrell weak at the knees. He'd make it good. Prep Aldric well first. And after... Images of him tending to the now-initiated Aldric, taking care of him, caressing him, flickered in his mind's eye.

Darrell being the big spoon to him all night. *The fuck?* He wasn't about that kind of thing. At *all*.

They were both silent for half the drive back to central San Antonio, Darrell at the wheel this time.

"You know, no one saw anyone attack that assistant with the nerd name. No one saw anyone in the alley or heard the stuff getting destroyed." Sean didn't look at Darrell as he spoke.

"So you think it could be a ghost? Like Buck Buckman's stuff is cursed? Oh. Maybe we should stop off at a church, get a man of the cloth's opinion? Even take him on as a consultant for the case?" Darrell kept up the act for a few more seconds before sniggering. "Sean, fuck's sake!" He'd needed that light relief. "Guess I'll pay the store a visit. Let them know Randa the widow will probably be burning up the phone lines, trying to buy back the items she sold them."

"Hey, with advance warning, they can tell her they got another buyer interested, jack up the re-sale prices. And if they do, they should cut you in for a piece."

"And me cut you in, yeah?" Darrell couldn't not laugh, partnering Sean. They had an easy relationship—mainly, Darrell thought, because they kept it easy. What would happen if he ever wanted to discuss anything more…difficult, with Sean? Darrell had the feeling he might not like the answer to that question.

* * * *

It was late morning before he could get to the store. He could have called, of course, but chose to go in person instead. He should apologize to Aldric. *Again.* The thought, the memory of what he needed to say sorry for, made him scowl. Why not call? Save himself the crap? It wasn't like he needed to gather more info or to corroborate anything to do with the case, and if he did, that could be obtained via the phone.

He caught a glimpse of Aldric through the glass window. Just a flash of dark hair and a twist of his slim body, and Darrell's hand was pushing open the door before his brain caught up with it. *Shit.* Well, he could and fucking well would be professional about this. The tinkling of the bells on the inside of the handle almost startled him.

"D-Darrell!" Aldric flushed a deep pink, and his eyes widened. He took a step back, knocking into a knee-high metal screen, then cast a quick look around. "Patrol Officer Williams, I mean. I didn't expect — What are you doing here?"

Aldric's rosy pink flush fascinated Darrell. *How far does it spread on his soft skin?* It dropped him into the middle of the pictures he'd been imagining, in which his actions, the delicious things he was doing to Aldric, caused Aldric's tan skin to take on that rose-pink color. It also confused him so much that he replied, "I had to see you."

Chapter Eight

"Oh, you did?" Aldric had rehearsed half a dozen things to say to Patrol Officer Darrell Williams if he ever crossed paths with him again, all of them as biting and savage as he could manage, and he hated that his lame comeback wasn't one of them.

He fought the heat that being in Darrell's presence again was kindling in him and that would be making his cheeks blush pink as a giveaway. He also forced himself not to move, rather than risk stumbling into anything. "Funny, when you couldn't hightail it out of my apartment quick enough the other night!"

Darrell didn't reply, and Aldric was petty enough to feel pleased that he'd silenced him. "What do you mean, *had* to see me?" he asked, because for sure the handsome cop hadn't been thinking about Aldric the way Aldric had been thinking about *him*. Aldric had been stoking and fanning the flames of indignation to combat the feelings of shame and inadequacy threatening to engulf him. As coping mechanisms went, it was lousy.

"I mean that I wanted to see you. To speak to you."

Footsteps behind Aldric told him Elliot was approaching. He hadn't told his boss or his co-worker what had happened after he'd left the hospital, of course, merely saying that Darrell had stayed until Aldric's cousin had arrived.

"Could we speak privately?" Darrell requested, addressing not only Aldric but Elliot now, sounding more like a cop and less like someone who'd told Aldric he wanted him and who had taken him.

"Yes, of course." Elliot sounded a little flustered by the blunt request. "Is there some news about what happened to Aldric?"

"Not here, please."

The store was far from crowded, with only a middle-aged couple browsing. Elliot had been on his way to attend to them when Darrell had entered.

"Jonas, could you…" Elliot gave a wave toward the old piano and the collection of sheet music on it that had attracted the couple. He received a nod in reply. "In my office?" He led the way to the back of the store. Aldric was used to the place now and it felt familiar to him, but he wondered what Darrell made of it. Would he ever get the chance to ask him?

Elliot was the first through the office door, and once behind his desk, he gestured to them to pull up chairs in the small room.

"Have you caught who did it? Is it known why Aldric was attacked?" Elliot demanded.

"No. No, sorry, I mean there's no new developments in that area at all." Darrell took out his notebook.

"Then why are you here?" Aldric almost shouted.

"I've just come from the Buckman estate, out at The Dominion," Darrell pivoted slightly, to include both Aldric and Elliot in his reply.

"I bought several items from there," Elliot immediately replied. "Is there a problem with one or more of them?"

"You bought items belonging to the late Buck Buckman. From his study?"

Elliot nodded. "I can show you. Several are displayed."

"There's been some vandalism up at the property. Broken windows and graffiti."

"Why are you telling us all this?" Aldric couldn't keep quiet any longer. "None of the things you're saying seem connected."

"Unless the officer is accusing us," Elliot said to Aldric, his tone one of disbelief.

"No, sir, I am not. Mrs. Buckman believes she shouldn't have sold certain things of her husband's that he liked a lot. Little puzzle boxes?"

"And *that's* not connected to anything else you've said, either," Aldric butted in. The sound of the piano being played out in the store and filtering through to the office seemed fitting—it was just as random as everything else Aldric was hearing.

"Mrs. Buckman's belief is that her late husband wants those small boxes, made of different-colored woods making mosaic patterns, returned to him, so he can be buried with them. If you'd like to speak to her, she'd be happy to take your call."

"She wants the stuff from the blind sale back?" Aldric was doing his best to get it straight and still didn't understand where the house being vandalized or the attack on him fitted in.

"But I bought the items fair and square!" Elliot opened a drawer, perhaps to look for the receipts, but closed it again. "And any shopkeeper buys goods intending to make a profit on them. The Buckman curios are excellent examples of smalls."

'"Smalls?"' Darrell asked.

"Small-sized vintage collectibles ideal for display cabinets and shelves," Aldric parroted. He'd been studying the store's reference books and guides every spare minute he got.

"Quite." Elliot gave him a proud beam. "Trinkets like that make very good walkout items."

"Let me guess, small things a customer can walk out of a store with?" Darrell asked.

"Aldric, you have a rival!" Elliot patted his desk.

Darrell had a nice smile, Aldric noticed. It made his green eyes lighten a shade and his freckles stand out, somehow.

"But all joking aside, Officer, Jonas, my other employee, has already started researching the curios collection and looking into possible points of resale, such as an upcoming auction in two weeks. He also has knowledge of collectors of similar artifacts whom we are planning to contact, to gauge their interest in buying. Thank you for your visit. Please let us know of developments in Aldric's case, should there be any. Now, if you'll excuse me, I have a store to run." Elliot stood, his dismissal clear, and Aldric and Darrell got to their feet too.

Darrell motioned Aldric out of the office ahead of him. A thought occurred to Aldric. "You don't think this Mrs. Buckman will come here and try to take those things, do you?"

Elliot marched past them before Darrell could answer. "Well, let's make it a little harder for her should she attempt that!" He crossed to the display table where Aldric, under his direction, had laid out the curios. Elliot liked to group goods by theme, so even though the oddities and curiosities were of different origin or date, they were set out together. Elliot picked up the wooden puzzle boxes, folding his arms to his chest to carry them all.

"I'm taking these to Sally," he called, so Jonas could hear.

"Is that another antiques trade term?" Darrell asked Aldric, who shook his head and beckoned Darrell closer to whisper.

"It's what Elliot calls the walk-in safe. The secure room with the keypad lock." He tilted his head to indicate the back of the store, from where they'd just come.

Darrell straightened, eyeing the customers. "And no need to let strangers know there's a safe on the premises."

"Yes." Aldric remembered he was mad at this man. *Damn my attraction.* "Well, I'd better get—"

"Lunch."

A carriage clock struck the time as Darrell spoke. Aldric held a finger up to shush him when he went to say more—the grandfather clock was about to bong too.

"Can I get you lunch?" Darrell said as soon as the echoes died. "I'd like to talk to you."

"To apologize?"

Darrell had turned up at the hospital to do just that, after his rudeness when they'd first met. And now this? Aldric was getting used to seeing patterns in his work here, and thought he detected another in his relationship with this man.

"To explain."

"Oh. I…doubt I can get free."

"Free? Yes, of course." Elliot, returning with empty arms, took out his pocket watch and compared it to the grandfather clock. "You need to take lunch."

"With Officer Williams," Aldric said. *Not sitting in the cramped kitchen here, eating a snack I bought from home, but out on a lunch date.* Because that was what it sounded like was happening.

"Fine. If that's fine with you?" Elliot raised an eyebrow.

"Yes. Yes it is." Aldric ducked a little to avoid anything with a reflective surface — he didn't want to see how big his grin was.

He didn't know any of the customers, not the older couple taking the sheet music that they'd chosen to the counter or the two younger women exclaiming over the amberina glass bowls, but Aldric felt they, along with Elliot and Jonas, watched him walk out with Darrell. It put a sway in his step. Or maybe that was all him.

There was no need to ask where they were going. The store was around the corner from the Pearl, that imposing gray building that formed one side of a huge plaza, the space attracting crowds for outdoor eating or just sitting around.

"Hey, look, isn't that the Big Red Taco Truck? I know it follows a route around the city, but it's here at this time? That's good to know." Darrell quickened his pace. "Come on!"

Aldric followed him through the animated lunchtime crowds and blinked in surprise to see that the short line of people waiting at the red truck's counter allowed Darrell to go ahead of them. He hung back, not knowing what to do — he wasn't a uniformed patrol officer, and it was highly unlikely anyone would mistake him for a plainclothes detective.

"Aldric?" Darrell beckoned. "I'm getting the puffy taco trio. You want the same?"

He'd never tried those, but the picture on the laminated menu displayed on the truck looked complicated. There were lots of things to drop and fall. Aldric was squeamish about eating in public, although getting a lot better with eating in front of Elliot, Jonas and even Meredith from the restaurant — she sometimes ate her lunchtime sandwich with him, saying their place was quieter and the company nicer.

"Er, could I get two fried cheese tacos, please? No garnish." He pointed to the photo, as if anyone needed to see the folded-over cheese-filled corn tortillas. The only risk there was the *queso blanco* and *queso panela* filling oozing out if he bit too hard.

"Better look for a bench," Darrell suggested when they had been served, juggling their paper taco trays and sodas. He was carrying Aldric's along with his own.

They found a vacant bench near the bike shop. "Thanks," Aldric said, taking and unwrapping his food carefully. He took a tentative nibble, the paper tray on his lap and his napkin at the ready near his chin. Darrell wasn't so reticent, taking huge bites and finishing half his Coke in one long swallow that Aldric tried not to track, even though the way the muscles of Darrell's strong throat worked was... He tried to think of the right adjective.

"Isn't it okay? Or not your usual choice?" Darrell pointed at Aldric's still mostly uneaten food. "You like to eat healthy? I do if I can. If not, I work out more." He sucked in shredded lettuce before it escaped. It should have looked icky, but the sweep of his tongue tip over his lips had Aldric fighting not to stare. "And I got no excuse, when there's a good gym in my apartment complex, and two pools, one on the roof."

"Not in mine," Aldric muttered. "As you might have noticed, when fleeing into the night. What was it that did it? How trigger-happy I was?"

Darrell put what remained of his food back into its container and placed that down between them. "It's not you."

"It's me." Aldric wasn't attempting a joke. He was one. Needy and nervous and no doubt more things beginning with *n. Nerd, for instance.*

"You can't doubt I find you sexy." Darrell lowered his voice although they were alone, and Aldric thought he began to understand Darrell's deal. "I can't take my eyes off that pert ass of yours."

"You mean you want to see me again?"

"I mean I'd like to fuck you, yeah." Darrell held the last remnants of his taco out for Aldric to taste. "You've never tried chili beef taco meat? It's good."

"Darrell?"

At the woman's voice, Darrell slammed his tray back onto the bench and stood. "*Brianna*? Do you work around here? I thought you worked with Leah?"

"Seeing a client." She pointed at the Pearl building. "I'm in a different field to Leah. It was great to meet your family the other day."

Darrell shot a glance at Aldric.

"I thought you might have called about the football game we were talking about? It sounds like fun. Go Lions!"

Aldric tried not to listen. Should he have walked away a little and given Darrell privacy? Introduced himself when the woman left a pause and looked at him? *No.* The meanie in him enjoyed seeing Darrell on the spot and trying to back away from it with committing himself. It seemed like he'd had a fair amount of practice at that.

"So," he said, when the short exchange was over, and the woman walked away.

"She works with my brother's girlfriend. No, fiancée now." Darrell sat, swallowed the remains of his food and balled up his paper napkin. "And got invited along to a get-together."

His family were fixing him up with girls? "You're bi?"

Darrell shook his head. "Not one bit."

"Ah." Aldric thought his suspicions must be correct. "They don't know." About *what*, he left blank.

"They're...traditional." Darrell sighed. "Military. Macho."

Aldric scoffed, indicating that Darrell filled out his uniform well.

"And the SAPD isn't exactly gay-friendly either." Darrell stood, grabbing his trash. "Things are...complicated all round. *This* is complicated. And I try to keep things simple."

"So why ask me to lunch?" Aldric stood too. He should head back. Head away from this, whatever it was, and not poke it like some idiot jamming a stick into a wasps' nest.

"I don't know." Darrell relieved Aldric of his garbage. "Except I wanted to."

"Want to walk me back to work?" Aldric wasn't above being a bitch. He made sure to be a little ahead, putting a sway into his hips to showcase his 'pert ass'. Thinking about returning to the store made him ask, "Is the vandalism of the Buckmans' house and what happened here at Intrinsic Value connected?"

"Randa Buckman thinks so. She thinks it's her husband's ghost," Darrell answered.

Aldric stumbled to a stop. "What? Like a *curse*?"

Darrell shrugged.

"Well, the store looks fine at the moment." Aldric peered up at the façade. "Maybe you should check the safe?" He didn't know exactly what he was doing, but he knew what he was hoping. Elliot was out, and Jonas a vague shape squatting to arrange something under the locked glass of the front counter. He didn't look up, so probably didn't even register Aldric hurrying in and to the back of the store with Darrell. *I hope.*

He keyed in the combination once he'd lifted the correct painting from the array on the wall next to the door to reveal the number pad, then shut the door behind the two of them in the narrow room that was little more than a cupboard.

"It all looks fine," Darrell began. The smile starting to inch up his face became wide-eyed surprise when Aldric's shove had him against the door.

"*You* kissed me last time," Aldric said, then brushed his mouth over Darrell's. He doubted he was as proficient, but when he flicked his tongue over Darrell's, Darrell opened for him, and the jalapeno heat, chipotle smoke and raw onion sting had Aldric's head swimming.

The murmur of surprised pleasure Darrell gave as Aldric tasted him rumbled through Aldric, building need and want. Darrell took over the kiss, pressing into Aldric before parting his legs with a strong thigh, making Aldric moan. The kiss turned as hard and desperate as the rut of their lower bodies that had their cocks rubbing against each other, until Darrell pulled off with a gasp.

"Aldric, that last time…"

Aldric's imagination took over with the rest of the sentence, aided by the friction of Darrell's taut muscles against his balls, demanding his arousal, then Darrell's hand between their bodies, palming his cock.

Darrell sliding down Aldric's body to kneel in front of him helped flesh things out more. Aldric found he was leaning against the door, needing its support as Darrell unfastened his pants and tugged them and his briefs down.

"Was then. *This* is this time," Darrell said — his only warning before he stroked Aldric's cock from root to tip then sucked the head.

Aldric shoved his hand into his mouth to hold in his whimper. The other hand he speared through Darrell's hair, for all that it was too short to grab. His hips bucked, pushing his dick deeper down Darrell's throat, and Darrell wrapped a hand around the base, stopping Aldric from thrusting too hard. When Darrell cupped Aldric's balls, Aldric had to use both hands to cover his mouth. This was intense. Darrell teasing and sucking, then suddenly taking him deep. More intense still was Darrell's fingers tip-tapping behind Aldric's balls to his ass, seeking, searching…

And finding. Darrell ran a fingertip around Aldric's tight pucker and pressed inward, just slightly. The mixture of that and how deep he took Aldric's cock dragged Aldric's climax from him, kicking and screaming. Well, he would have been if Darrell hadn't been holding his thighs, and if he wasn't biting down on the back of his own hand hard enough to leave teeth marks in his flesh. The noise he made as he shot his hot cum down Darrell's throat sounded as loud as thunder, filling each corner of the small room.

"S-stop," Aldric begged when Darrell kept swallowing and didn't let up the pressure on his hole, and it took a nudge from his trembling knee to make Darrell pull off. "Get up."

Again, he didn't know what he was going to do until he did it, until his hand found Darrell's erect dick, straining at his zipper. His fingers tangled with Darrell's, undoing the fastener and releasing Darrell. He was huge, and Aldric raised startled eyes to Darrell's, finding them fixed on him, which was somehow more personal than Darrell blowing him. Aldric just about managed to close his fingers around Darrel's shaft when a noise came from just outside the door—someone calling Aldric's name.

"This is crazy." Darrell half-turned and zipped himself up—carefully. "I have to go."

"Darrell." Aldric's voice stopped him. "I understand. You're not in the right place mentally for a real relationship." He swallowed. "Neither am I, but what I am is brave enough to try. I won't be a dirty little secret."

Darrell looked down, then back up at Aldric again. "I know."

He slipped from the room and was gone. Aldric waited a minute then followed, seeing Darrell's back view vanishing through the shop door.

Aldric had meant it. He wanted Darrell, and he meant to have him. Fully.

Chapter Nine

Darrell stifled a curse and threw himself back in his chair when the latest image he opened didn't match either. "How good is this damn database anyway?" he asked no one in particular.

Only Officer Lind replied, crossing on his way to the few filing cabinets the station still had. "Can't go wrong with paper, I always say."

The screech of the little-used metal cabinet drawer being forced open jangled Darrell's nerves. He half-opened his mouth to tell the older officer he really had to get to grips with the wonderful world of IT but closed it. Lind knew that. It didn't mean he'd do it, though, if he could put it off until retirement.

It wasn't Lind making him edgy, anyway. It was the fact that Darrell hadn't been able to find any information on the graffiti tag that had been sprayed outside Intrinsic Value sometime over the course of last night, and which he'd observed this morning. He'd driven past the store just like he had yesterday, with his vague reasoning behind it being *look out for Aldric.*

Okay, so Darrell didn't know if that meant *protect him* or *try to catch a glimpse of him*.

He hadn't seen Aldric, but had noticed the new graffiti, and waited for Elliot to show up to make the report. *A pentagram. Who the fuck spray-paints pentagrams?* The same person who'd sprayed the security camera lens black and who'd drawn a weird-looking coffin along with the pentagram, he supposed. Not that the sergeant cared, about either a possible new tagger or problems at an antique store. The crime wasn't deemed a serious case, not with the amount of graffiti sprayed in that area, so there was no chance of handing it off to a detective. When Darrell had asked Fuentes what he was waiting for—another attack on a staff member there, perhaps—the man had replied, "*Yeah*".

So yeah, maybe when a different employee was attacked, Fuentes would connect the dots. Darrell squinted hard at the rectangle shape. Was it a coffin? It could be a box. And if so—

"Hey." Sean slid behind his desk opposite Darrell, breaking into his thoughts.

Darrell sat straighter. "Anything?" He kept his voice quiet.

Sean shook his head. "Negative. Both those kids seem like your regular accidental Good Samaritans. I think they're clean. No record at their school either."

"And it would be too much to hope for that they remembered any other pertinent information," Darrell muttered. "I can't match that symbol to any known gang." One of the reason Fuentes had turned his back on it.

"I'd normally say it's a wanna-be. A toy." Sean liked to be up on the latest expressions, the opposite of Lind.

"But with that, you could be better off looking up local cults."

"Like Satanists?" Darrell was scornful but did it anyway. Well, he had the internet right there. "A pentagram's an occult symbol used to convey a curse?" he read out, not believing.

Sean shrugged. "Worth seeing if we can hand it over now?"

Darrell considered the question. They didn't have much more than they'd had — he didn't want to get kicked back twice in one morning. But the least he could do was pass that nugget on, and not to Fuentes. He headed for the break room, but the fresh pot of coffee had drawn a few officers there, chatting as they filled their mugs, making him about-face into the kids' interview room. It wasn't used that much, so although it wasn't big, it tended to be private. He sat at one of the small tables and called the store.

"Intrinsic Value. Elliot speaking. How may I help you?" came smooth, old-fashioned tones not belonging to Aldric.

Darrell held in a sigh. "It's Officer Williams. No, there's no news. I — "

"Yes, hello, Officer," came the pointed reproach.

Now he did sigh, shifting on the child-sized chair. "Sorry to be abrupt. Okay, what I'm about to say's gonna sound a little out there." He launched into what Randa believed about her husband's ghost haunting the place — she'd even used the word *curse* — and how a pentagram indicated that same thing. "I'm not saying I buy into this, of course," he cautioned. He'd made a pile of the red plastic blocks on the table in front of him, and now started on the white ones.

"Well, thank you, Officer," Elliot replied at last. "Please don't concern yourself with looking this up any further. I have my own expert here researching into this. Oh, and I received a call from a Ms. Guyler, the assistant of Randa Buckman."

"Wanting the items back?" Darrell stirred his finger through the plastic blocks, mixing them up again. "But you won't." The guy was quiet but firm and had a stubborn streak. Who did that remind Darrell of?

"No. I'm not inclined to. Not even when the lady herself took the phone and ordered me to 'name my price', then sobbed hysterically when I wouldn't."

Darrell guessed being haunted would do that to a widow. "That's up to you, sir. Look, I have no idea what, if anything, is going on, but it seems someone wants those puzzle boxes," he warned.

"Yes and that's the reason I'm moving all the Buckman objects to the safety deposit warehouse."

"Not your safe, you don't mean?"

No, Elliot didn't. His short description of the warehouse location, out past the north side of town but before the Hill Country, piqued Darrell's interest. San Antonio had a couple of companies doing that, competing with banks to store goods such as safe deposit boxes and larger items…without all the compliance checks most banks were mandated to carry out. *Interesting.* Darrell made a mental note to look into Mr. Elliot Douglas.

"Oh, one moment." A faint, muffled exchange took place on the other end of the phone. "May I put Aldric on?"

Before Darrell could reply, the sound of a door closing reached him through the phone line, followed by a gulped intake of breath. "Darrell?"

Just the sound of his name in Aldric's voice had him shifting again, and not because of the comically too-small chair this time. He'd jacked off that morning, but his dick was waking up and taking notice now. "Yeah. Yeah, I'm here," he interrupted Aldric, who was saying his name again, with hesitation in his tone.

"Would you like to go out on a date?"

He'd expected Aldric to ask some question about the graffiti, to be scared shitless about the pentagram, so Aldric's actual question sent him reeling. Aldric's voice was quiet, almost timid, but the determination rang through. That combination had Darrell's balls tightening.

"If you don't, that's —"

"No! Yeah. Yeah, I do." *Oh. It seems I do.* "You got anything in mind? Anywhere, I mean." His brain worked at double speed to make up for his spacy-ness.

"Not exactly. And I don't have a car."

"I'll plan something. And I'll pick you up."

They arranged a time, and Darrell blew out a breath as he disconnected. He didn't do dates with guys. Never had. But…he wanted to, with Aldric. He started thinking about the where and the what of it, and a smile took over his face.

* * * *

"I'd never been in a pickup truck until this one," Aldric confessed, settling into the passenger seat of Darrell's Tacoma.

"Yeah?" Darrell jerked his chin to remind Aldric to put the seat belt on. He'd had to do that when he'd taken Aldric home from the hospital but had put that down to the accident and the meds. Now, though, he understood there was another reason Aldric wasn't so familiar with vehicles. "What would you get, if you were in the market for a car?"

"If I drove, I'd get a Tesla." Aldric peered down at the dashboard. "They're EV, so better for the planet, and the Model S is so cool!"

Aldric didn't drive? Was that what he meant? Darrell was trying to figure out his words and almost missed a question. "Huh? Oh, dinner and a movie. All in one." He grinned and hoped Aldric would like what he had planned.

Aldric seemed to. When they reached the drive-in, his eyes were wide as he looked around, taking it all in. "Why are you backing in?" he asked.

He didn't ask why Darrell was parking behind all the other vehicles, right up against the rock marking the end of the lot. *Not that naïve, then.* "So we can relax in the bed. Here, make yourself useful and tune the FM into the station it says on the program, and I'll go get us dinner."

Well, hotdogs and chips. Jeez, his nutrition flew out of the window around Aldric. When he reached the truck again, he beckoned for Aldric to hop out of the cab and join him in the back. "There's beer in the cooler." The drive-in didn't sell it. "And water." He wasn't trying to get Aldric drunk.

"What's a Buddy-Buddy Season?" Aldric ran his finger along the title in the printed program.

"Classic cop movies, from the seventies onward, that they're showing all month. Double bills. See?"

"*The French Connection. Freebie and the Bean.* They sound interesting choices, especially for an off-duty police officer." Aldric smiled.

Darrell didn't have time to worry that Aldric wouldn't enjoy them, just as he didn't have to worry about his poor food choices. Not when, a half-hour into the first movie, their dinner was abandoned, and they had no attention to spare for the screen. How could any movie, no matter how classic or award-winning, compete with Aldric's body under his, and Darrell's lips over Aldric's? How could any musical score sound as entrancing as Aldric's gasps when Darrell's tongue invaded his mouth, dominating his?

The sounds of surrender Aldric made and the yielding of his body had Darrell hard and more demanding in response, nipping at Aldric's lips and parting his thighs with a knee. Aldric kissing back, attempting to seize control, had Darrell groaning and sliding a hand down to cup Aldric's balls and show him just who was in charge. Aldric's response wasn't to roll Darrell over, slamming him into the floor of the truck that Darrell had covered with a picnic blanket. No, he sighed and tilted his head back, exposing the soft skin of his throat and neck.

Oh yeah. Darrell took him up on the invitation—a much better one than his lame movie-night idea. He sucked at a patch of skin there, sensitizing it for his nip seconds later, and the intake of breath Aldric made in response rasped out into the night air.

"Shh." Darrell continued soothing with his tongue, easing away any remaining sting, then nibbled again, harder. He got off on kissing a man's throat, at the amount of trust it took for a person to let a partner play there, and this time sucked deep enough to leave a mark.

And all the time, Aldric cupped the nape of Darrell's neck, scratching into his short hair, giving him as much access as he wanted to that smooth, warm skin. Except, it wasn't as much as he wanted. It couldn't be, here, like this.

"Aldric." Darrell sat up.

A little dazed, Aldric copied him.

"This" — Darrell indicated the truck, the drive-in — "isn't working."

That flush took over Aldric's face again. He looked down. "What did I—?"

"No." Darrell wouldn't let him think for one second anything was wrong. "I mean this here, making out like teenagers. We went further than this last time, and that taste of you I got, when I sucked your cock? That wasn't enough either." He waited for Aldric to react, but Aldric remained quiet, his eyes as round as saucers.

"So…" Aldric whispered at last, his breath barely making it past his lips.

"So I want to take you home with me, so I can fuck you. Jesus, do I need that ass." Darrell paused, watching that sexy flush wash an even darker pink over Aldric's face, like the tide had come in. "Can't wait any fucking longer to have you." The way Aldric bit down on his lower lip told Darrell he might like filthy talk. *Hmm. Something to put to the test…* "You can say no."

"No." Aldric spoke before Darrell could clarify. "No, I mean I'm not saying no. I'm saying yes."

His hectic pink blush had faded a little and his eyes were still huge, but the tiny smile on Aldric's face was no longer quite as timid as it had been. In fact, curiosity and wickedness bracketed its edges, and Darrell's dick stiffened in response. *Fuck*, he was gonna enjoy this.

Chapter Ten

Darrell lived on the Broadway Corridor, part of the Pearl District, so Aldric could almost feel he was going back to work. He didn't know the area very well, sticking to the streets close to the store. The huge, sprawling multi-building complex where Darrell entered through a barrier and pulled into a covered parking space came as a surprise. The development was as big as a university campus, with breezy courtyards between buildings and spacious outdoor walkways connecting them. He didn't quite know how he felt about it.

"You said there was a gym?" He tried to make conversation while they walked.

"And a couple of pools." Darrell paused in his loping stride, as if going to change direction and take Aldric on a tour.

"No." Aldric gathered all his courage and put a hand on Darrell's arm. "I don't want to see the complex. I'd rather see you." His face was hot with a blush and his hands were on the verge of trembling, but that wasn't going to stop him.

"Good." Darrell grinned. "Because I'd rather *lick* you all over. I love how you taste. We're here."

There was no comparison between Aldric's studio and Darrel's apartment—well, the bit of it Aldric saw as Darrell nudged him into the bedroom.

"Race ya," Darrell offered, pulling at his clothes. He was naked in seconds, and Aldric gulped, looking at his cock. It was thick as it hung semi-soft, and much thicker and longer as it grew erect.

"You really shouldn't look at me like that."

Darrell's words had Aldric raising his gaze to his. "Like…?"

"Like you want me to undress you." When Aldric said nothing, Darrell did just that. "And touch you." Aldric's body had the bare minimum of muscle definition, but Darrell traced a lot of them, leaving pebbled skin where his finger stroked. When Darrell reached one side of the vee muscle leading to Aldric's groin, Aldric's erect cock jumped. Pre-cum shone at the slit.

"I'll get you off first, so I can take my time with you after." Darrell didn't make it sound like a chore—more like a treat. When he curled a hand around Aldric's neck and pulled him in to kiss, it was as if Aldric were a candy he wanted to savor—and suck, taking up where he'd left off earlier, then making his way south.

His knees bent, as though he were about to fall to them, but he straightened, reversed direction and walked Aldric to the bed. When the backs of Aldric's knees hit the frame, he crumpled onto the mattress behind him, and Darrell was on him in a flash. Between them, they got Aldric situated to Darrell's satisfaction.

For the first time, Aldric felt Darrell's dick against his skin, and he shuddered, both at the heat of arousal and the thought of that big cock inside him. Turned on and daunted, he bucked into Darrell's hand.

"Someone's eager," Darrell commented. "Apart from me, that is. Gotta have a taste." He bent low and laved the head of Aldric's cock before taking it deep for a few heart-jolting seconds. When he pulled off, licking his lips, he glanced up at Aldric. "Your turn. Show me."

Aldric wrapped a hand around his dick, a little uncertain. *Show me* probably meant *show off for me*, and he wasn't sure he could. But when Darrell squeezed his fingers around Aldric's, making the foreplay instantly more erotic, Aldric jacked his shaft and needy moans fell from his lips without further prompting. His thumb and Darrell's rubbed over the head, spreading the pre-cum that was slick and shiny there.

When Darrell got a grip of his own dick, replicating the strokes they were both making on Aldric's, Aldric lost it. "*Shit!*" he hissed. "I can't—"

"Let yourself go," Darrell commanded. "Keep your eyes on me." He stopped working himself, as if to pay extra attention to Aldric, jacking him from root to tip, the pressure harder than Aldric usually liked on his own, but one he loved under Darrell's hand.

He cried out, thrusting up one final time into the constriction they both made around his dick, and most of his muscles, as undefined as they were, clenched as he came, gushing over his chest. His release was longer than usual, the world whiting out all around him and Darrell still stroking him, prolonging matters.

"Stop," Aldric whispered, hyper-sensitive, and Darrell stilled his hand, but left it around Aldric's deflated shaft.

"Look at you." Darrell swiped a finger through the cum cooling on Aldric's flesh. "Your cum all over your chest and belly. And you are so fucking sexy when you come. Can't wait to see what you look like taking my dick in that cute ass of yours." He pumped himself, two long, easy strokes. "One thing's for sure—I'm gonna get you even messier." He paused, his forehead creasing. "What?"

"I didn't say anything." Aldric was amazed he got his voice working. His heart was thundering and his nerves zinging. *This is it.*

"Aldric, is there anything you want to tell me?" Darrell asked slowly.

"Like..." Aldric couldn't pretend. "Like that I haven't done this before? This is my first time?" He dropped his gaze to the mess on his torso. He wasn't looking at Darrell but could tell from the movement of the bed that Darrell had moved away. Well, what did he expect? Aldric the freak, who had never been with another guy in all his twenty—

"Yeah. Exactly like that." Darrell was there again with a handful of Kleenex, dabbing at Aldric's chest. He sat back. "Well, *fuck me.* How did I get so lucky?"

When Aldric lifted his gaze to Darrell's face, the grin on it was blinding.

"I love going slow and taking my time, and that's not something many—" Darrell shook his head. "To get to savor you, to spend as long as I want, as long as you need, getting you ready...that's a gift I've not been given before." The kiss Darrell took Aldric's lips in was almost reverent. "You're really something."

Aldric agreed. *Something as in scared. Nervous. Wondering how much pain there'll be.*

"You're gonna love this. Be begging for more. Wondering how you got through life without a cock up your ass." Darrell's grin was promising now. "But you play with yourself, right? Toys, dildos?"

"Just my fingers."

"Shit, that image is *hot*." Darrell gave a long stroke to his cock as if in illustration. "Turn over so I can prep you. Gonna eat you out, hon."

Aldric rolled onto his stomach, his heart speeding with each thing Darrell informed him he was going to do for Aldric. *To me.* So when Darrell ran his nails down Aldric's back then smoothed his hands over his ass, Aldric almost squealed.

"Shhh," Darrell murmured. "I'll be gentle."

The nuzzle at his neck was, the nip that followed less so, but it made Aldric's entire body pulse. Pressure on his butt cheeks had them parting, exposing his hole, and the soft trail of wet warmth along it could only have been Darrell's tongue. *Oh. My. God. Rimming.* He'd read about it, of course, and seen videos, but now Aldric's whole world narrowed to that one spot made super-sensitive because Darrell's tongue was bringing every nerve ending in it to red-hot life.

"You're tighter because you just came," Darrell said behind him, the words puffing air across his now damp pucker. "So gonna lick you loose."

The wriggle Aldric gave was him trying to rut into the bed *and* press back against Darrell's tongue. He grabbed at the sheet, his hands curling into fists on either side of him. The noise that came from his throat was pure impatience.

"Hey." Darrell sounded amused. "Takes as long as it takes."

It took long, slow minutes of sweet torture before Darrell gave a final swipe and paused, and Aldric wondered where he'd moved to. Noises a second later explained it—to reach across to the nightstand for lube. This time the foreign object at Aldric's hole was harder, rounded and slippery, and Aldric clamped shut against it. Against Darrell's cock wanting in.

"Sorry," he gasped.

"Not a problem. We'll take all the time you need," Darrell assured him, and ran the tip of his finger in a tight circle around Aldric's pucker, keeping the nerve endings there firing and also kindling tiny fires in Aldric's bloodstream.

Aldric didn't know whether it was Darrell's touch or his murmurs of praise that had him relaxing, but within a minute, the tip of Darrell's finger was in him. There was a squirt of viscous gel, not warmed, and Darrell pushed farther, until Aldric was clenching around it. "Is that it? Is it in?" he asked.

Darrell's chuckle was dirty. "To the first knuckle, yeah. Push back for me, babe."

The endearment registered more than the instructions, but when they did, Aldric got his knees working, to give him leverage to press back as directed, and bore down on the intrusion in his ass, chasing it when Darrell pulled out. This time when Darrell penetrated him again, it was with something thicker, larger, and Aldric moaned. "Two?" He tightened around them.

"Yeah, and you took them like a champ. Let's see…"

Darrell seeing didn't seem to involve him moving, so, impatient for more sensation, Aldric took the initiative. He began rocking forward and back, the stretch to his hole and his ass making him press his face into the sheet. It also had him craving more.

"You're a natural," Darrell assured him. "Wish you could see how goddamn sexy you look, fucking yourself on my hand." He shifted position, and the thick, wet-tipped press of his cock on Aldric's thigh was no longer threatening, but a next step. "Think you can take another?"

Most of Aldric's nod ended up in the mattress cushioning him, but Darrell must have caught enough to ease free and return with an even thicker penetration that stretched Aldric's rim and his walls as Darrell pushed inside slowly. Aldric realized he was holding his breath and forced it out.

"Jesus, your ass is amazing!"

A swat across one cheek had him opening his mouth to scream, but what emerged was a moan of pleasure.

Darrell's, "*Oh*," held a world of pleased discovery in it. "I think that's enough warm-up. If you've never felt *this* before, it's gonna blow your mind."

"This—*sshiiittt!*" Aldric's hiss turned into a scream as Darrell massaged his prostate. His instinct was to pull away, but Darrell moved his fingers like they were a part of him, rubbing with purpose. Sparks snapped into being behind his eyelids, and he half-curled onto his side while curse words he rarely used fell from his lips in a stream—*Jesus* and *God* and *fuck* and *shit* loud among them.

Seconds later, his fetal scrunch became a writhe, Aldric pierced by bolts of scorching-hot ecstasy. First localized, they soon radiated through him, making him shake under their onslaught, and he was amazed that Darrell stayed with him, never ceasing to stroke his gland and engulf him in obscene pleasure.

"Holy fuck. I've never had anyone take to it like this. And if you're like that with a little press of the finger on the prostate, what the hell are you gonna do when I get my dick in you?" The *little press* that had become a *right-there* rub was now a slow drag, and Aldric saw stars.

What will I do? Scream. Faint. Die, probably. In the meantime, he pushed and strained, fucking himself on Darrell's merciless fingers that twisted and caressed and stretched, with the knowledge that Darrell was waiting to slide his erect cock in to plow his ass only adding to the thrill.

When Darrell pulled free, leaving him empty, it was like the world paused. Rather than sob out a question about the sudden emptiness he felt, Aldric looked back in blurry confusion and caught Darrell's mutter of, "Condom." *Oh. Of course.* Mesmerized, Aldric watched the glide of Darrell's hand down his length, saw how the spread of lubrication left his cock glistening.

"Got to make sure there's enough." Darrell added more. "Don't wanna hurt you."

Aldric faced front again a second before something thicker pressed at his hole. He didn't have time to make an answer to Darrell's quick, "Ready?" before his massive cock breached Aldric's ring, and all the breath slammed from his lungs.

Darrell had enough breath, though, if the low groan he released was an indication. "Je-*sus*, Aldric! I wish you knew how good you feel. Warm and tight and *incredible*. That's one…"

One…stretch? Burn? Ache? Penetration? All of the above? Aldric didn't know what Darrell meant and couldn't stop the half-hiccup, half-wheeze that forced its way up his throat at the fear that it was too much already.

"Breathe," Darrell instructed. "I need to go deeper. You got a second set of muscles in there, you know. Push down."

The noise that Aldric made sounded inhuman to his own ears as he thrust his hips back to accept all of Darrell. He was scared, yes, but craved the fat head of Darrell's dick on that place inside him that had drowned him in a wave of pleasure. Except...*too much.*

"Thisthe..." *Second stage, you said?* he wanted to ask but couldn't get his voice or thoughts in a row to do so. Then he didn't have to, not when he felt that hard slide within him, as if through a place where he were tighter, where he gripped harder. No, no need to ask — the soul-wrenched groan Darrell made at forging deeper told him.

"You okay?" Darrell had paused and his voice seemed to come from a distance — it took a while to register, at least.

When Aldric understood Darrell was checking in on him, he nodded, which was when Darrell pushed farther still. "Shit," Darrell breathed. "All the fucking way. I'm fully inside you, babe."

Taking Darrell that deep hurt and Aldric bucked, nearly dislodging him. He panted like an animal, with his hands curled almost painfully against the mattress.

"Wait — I'll pull out."

And the drag of Darrell's cock along Aldric's nerve-rich inner walls made supernovas burst into life. Sounds of wonder issued from him, comprehensible enough for Darrell to reply to by plunging back inside, to bottom out, again. The scrape over Aldric's prostate as he did so had Aldric unraveling at the seams. He sank down on his chest a little and turned his head to the side to watch Darrell's face.

"You're beautiful." Darrell said what Aldric was thinking. "Your ass was made for my cock." Okay, he hadn't been thinking quite that. "Can't fucking believe I can get so deep in you your first time." He rocked his hips into Aldric's ass, slow-fast, fast-slow, time and again, sweat dripping from him.

His slap to Aldric's ass had Aldric's dick trying to stir, much to Aldric's disbelief. He'd just come, and he'd never climaxed twice in one session. He shoved until he could get a hand to his shaft when rubbing it against the sheet wasn't enough. He had no cum left in him, and his erection wasn't a full one. He was glad about that—he preferred to focus on what Darrell was doing to his ass. Darrell twisted down to drop a kiss on Aldric's lips, and Aldric rose a little to meet him.

That weird position must have contorted his channel—Darrell made a strangled, bitten-off sound and jerked his hips in short, rough prods. He gave a final long thrust and stayed there, buried deep with his body tight. Sudden hotness burst in Aldric's ass that he could feel even through the condom.

A smaller, spikier ecstasy slapped Aldric, brought on by Darrell stroking over his gland and his own hand rubbing just under the head of his cock. It whited out the world for thick, ringing seconds then faded, leaving him drained, but probably not as much as Darrell, who collapsed on top of him with a grunt. *If I can't move, for sure he can't.*

"*Fuck!*" Darrell breathed, easing out and rolling to the side. Exhilaration shone from his gleaming-red face. "That was fucking *perfect*. You're okay?"

Aldric managed a nod, trying to make sense of what Darrell was saying about a condom, figuring it out when Darrell left the bed and the room. He jumped at the warm softness touching him—Darrell back with a washcloth. Aldric obediently moved and stretched, following Darrell's directions, until he was clean.

"You know you'll be sore." Darrell got in beside him, moving him over and arranging him.

Aldric nodded. "You'll be here." Of course Darrell would. This was his place.

As if his thought had poked something in Darrell, he looked startled, glancing down at where his arm was stealing over Aldric's chest. "I never…" He swallowed.

"No. *I* never." Aldric tried to stay awake, reliving the sensations. He still felt the throb of Darrell in his ass. But he couldn't and, nestling into Darrell, he fell asleep.

Chapter Eleven

The half-snore that got trapped in his throat and found its way out in a hard, painful exhalation woke Darrell. He was immediately aware that something was different…that someone else was in his apartment. On autopilot, he went for his gun in the drawer of his nightstand before he remembered.

Aldric stayed the night.

Aldric. Aldric Beamer. Darrell risked a look at him, where he lay sleeping by his side. The daylight streaming in allowed Darrell to see that his fluff of brown hair was even more tousled and his face was softer and younger as he slept. Or maybe that was because he wasn't wearing his glasses. Darrell didn't know what to do about the situation. About the guy who he hadn't been able to stop thinking about since he'd seen him in that alley, injured, his glasses askew and his sweet face twisted in pain and bewilderment and tugging at Darrell's heartstrings. The caring Darrell had felt had left him as confused as Aldric had looked, and Aldric had suffered a knock to his head, for fuck's sake.

"Hey."

Darrell almost jumped. "You okay? I can get you something. What do you need? How do you feel?"

The hand Aldric reached out to him landed heavily on his arm. "Good morning. I feel fine. I slept well."

Darrell had too. "Okay. That's good."

"And in case you got me confused with one of the artifacts in the store, I'm not made of glass. I didn't and I won't shatter."

The feeble joke made Darrell smile. A little.

"I'm starving, though. Need some breakfast." Aldric took his glasses from the nightstand then swung his legs to the floor and stood a little carefully. He walked around the bed slowly, as if testing himself. "Your shift starts later, you said?"

The subtext hit Darrell over the head. "You're a pushy bottom."

"Oh." Aldric considered. He looked away for only a second before his brown-eyed gaze was drilling into Darrell. "What about if I let you choose the place? Or didn't you say this apartment complex has restaurants or whatever, but food, on the bottom level?"

One hell of a pushy bottom, Darrell thought later, still not quite understanding how it had happened, but finding himself walking with Aldric down the stairs to the food court. "Here's fine." At least Darrell supposed the kiosk, with its drinks and snacks that the customers ate standing around the high tables, was good. He usually grabbed what he wanted from the cart on his side of the complex, nearer his exit.

"No donuts?" Aldric asked, when Darrell put a protein bar down with their drinks and Aldric's pastry.

"I don't always eat crap." Darrell went on the defensive before Aldric's face clued him in. "Oh. Cop equals donuts. Got it. Woah, you are hungry."

He waited for Aldric to blush, but if he did, it was hidden by the Danish he was stuffing into his mouth.

"I didn't eat dinner," Aldric reminded him, a little indistinctly.

"Shouldn't be so tempting then," Darrell told him, his grin making it hard to drink whatever the fruit and yogurt blend of the day in his to-go cup was.

"But I liked the date." The twinkle in Aldric's eyes encouraged Darrell to loosen up a bit more.

"The movie?" Darrell could play too. He kept his expression one of mild confusion.

Aldric snorted softly, and his smile dimmed. "We can't leave it there, you know."

He should have expected the squeeze to his chest those words gave. He breathed in, hoping his sly glances all around for listening ears were unobtrusive. Jesus, he owed Aldric after last night, owed him more than loaning him the olive-green Henley and sweatpants he was wearing after showering in Darrell's bathroom. Alone. Darrell had wanted to go check on Aldric, see how his head wound was looking, for instance, but hadn't trusted himself to go in.

Another element was that Darrell didn't exactly want to leave it there either, and Aldric had made it clear he wasn't just someone Darrell could call up for a fuck. But what came next? Lunch? Dinner? Taking Aldric to watch the football game? He settled on a grunt that could have conveyed *I know*.

"Yes. There are three more decades of buddy-cop movies to go, if I remember the program correctly."

"You little…" Darrell nearly spluttered out his green juice. "Got any plans for the morning?"

"Oh. I've been thinking." Aldric wiped his hands on a napkin, having finished his Danish.

Darrell looked at his protein bar. It wasn't nearly as appetizing as what Aldric had eaten. "I get the feeling you do that a lot. Go on?"

"About what sort of person this Buck Buckman guy was."

This was so far removed from anything Darrell had expected Aldric to say that he blinked in surprise. "Buck? He was one of the richest guys in SA. His retail estate consortium had a hand in developing this Broadway Corridor and the Riverwalk, among other projects. That I do know." He swirled the thick, globby dregs of his juice in the clear cup.

"Yes. I looked at some articles. And he was a benefactor to the city's cultural heritage. He donated to the San Antonio River Foundation." Aldric gestured to where the river ran. "If it wasn't for him, we wouldn't have the River of Lights in December."

"All those lights in the trees and on the bridges?" It was pretty. Darrell had done a little reading up of his own after meeting Randa Buckman, but mainly about the family and Buck's company, Amgine.

"And in the water. He wanted those." Aldric screwed his napkin into a ball. "So with the reflections, the water looks twice as bright as the banks. Like a trick."

"Or a joke."

Aldric nodded and helped himself to the last corner of Darrell's protein bar. "And he made a lot of donations to the art museum. I thought I'd go look at what he gave them, see if I can understand what kind of man he was. Maybe it'll help with the case. The vandalism and all that."

That being the supposed curse or haunting. Darrell didn't have the heart to tell Aldric that the assault he'd suffered plus the graffiti to a mid-range antique store hardly constituted a priority case to the detective handling it for the SAPD. There'd been no high-value robbery, and Intrinsic Value was not what could be called a high-level target.

"Or I could just go work in the store. It's my Saturday off, but there's always something to do there." Aldric mumbled the last bit into the silence Darrell had left.

"Or, who better than to help you be a detective than an actual police officer?" Darrell grinned, loving how Aldric's shy smile in answer spread into a wide, joyous one that took over his face.

"I was planning to walk there, along the path to the museum stretch. It's pretty beside the river." Aldric breathed on his glasses and rubbed the lenses with the hem of his Henley.

"That so?" Darrell guided him as they left the food kiosk and turned so that they'd leave the residential complex by the exit that came out near the riverbank. He paused. "There's a bike rental right here in the complex, two walkways along from mine, if you want to ride."

Again he surprised himself. He'd be packing them a little picnic next. Oh, wait. He'd kind of done that last night, right? *Last night.* He caught up with what he'd just suggested, after what he'd done last night. Aldric had taken his first cock. His virgin ass had been tight — and not to boast, but Darrell was a good size. The last thing the newly fucked Aldric needed was to sit on a narrow bike seat, for shit's sake.

"Or the kayak rental station is just over there," he continued. "Do you kayak? I haven't done it in a while. It's great exercise."

"I like walking. You like sports, right?"

"What gave me away, all the equipment in my apartment?"

"And the trophies. I noticed them this morning."

Yeah, last night they'd been in too much of a rush to take in the finer points of his interior décor. "I grew up in a family of sports nuts. Competing was mandatory." Mention of his family made him keep a look-out as they walked down the steps to the walkway alongside the river. Although it wasn't likely any of them would be here, downtown, on a Saturday morning, and the thought of any of them anywhere near a museum was laughable.

"You said your family was traditional. Military, you mentioned?"

We're at the 'tell me about your family' stage? Darrell considered brushing the question off like he would have with a hook-up, but Aldric wasn't that. He wasn't a one-and-done. The urge to answer him truthfully was impossible to fight off. "Yes. My father was a decorated Battlefield Airman in Special Reconnaissance, then was asked to help develop and run some of the training courses at Lackland. It's his tenth year doing that now. My older brother followed in his footsteps, as hard as that is, as Chief—my father—has big shoes to fill. Well. That's what we've been hearing ever since we were kids. Travis, my brother, he's just joined the Night Stalkers. And my younger brother— Oh, you get the picture."

"So you're the rebel."

"Not 'the middle child'? The 'odd one'?" He did the quote marks.

"Family labels." Aldric's lips thinned. "Like, 'afterthought'. Or 'surprise baby'."

He gets it. Darrell nodded, quick and tight. So there was a generation gap and a half between Aldric and his parents? *They must be a helluva lot older.* And yet, Darrell would have bet Aldric could probably bring a guy home to them, as a boyfriend or significant other, something *he'd* never be able to. He hardened his heart and nodded at the fortress-like dark brown building up the grassy slope, on the landscaped lawn. *Looks like a fort and was a former brewery. San Antonio in a nutshell.*

"I haven't been here since a school trip," he confessed as they walked in through the metal detector. A flash of his badge got him his gun and all the metal contents of his pockets back, unlike Aldric, who had to exchange his huge bunch of keys for a reclaim ticket. Darrell looked for the entrance desk. "And I can't remember any of it."

"It's probably changed since then, anyway. They get new artworks all the time."

"And new rooms," Darrell said, spotting a sign for a space bearing the name *Buckman Room*. "Is all the stuff he gave in one place?"

"No, I don't think so. Look." Aldric indicated the list of donors in the program he'd just bought. "Seems he's given paintings to several collections. Want to go on a trail, find all the donations he made? It's not canoeing or off-roading, but..." He'd ducked away before Darrell could protest that he wasn't just some knuckle-dragging jock and he did in fact like culture.

He might like it, but he didn't think he understood it, or any kind of connection between the pictures the late Mr. Buckman had gifted the place. He and Aldric traipsed from nineteenth and twentieth century European art to American, and Darrell admitted defeat. The most he could come up with was that the art looked sort of three-dimensional.

"You know how macho guys think it's a sign of weakness to look at the instructions when they're building something or putting something together?" he asked. "Call me a nerd, but I'd better see the specs on this." He studied the relevant paragraph. "Oh, Jesus. I can't even pronounce this."

"Me neither. But it's explained, see?" Aldric pointed lower down the page and his finger brushed Darrell's thumb. It felt good.

"'Deceive the eye'." Darrell almost fist-pumped in triumph. "I *thought* three-D! 'Realistic imagery creates optical illusions that depict objects existing in three dimensions.'"

"It really does." Aldric indicated the hundred-year-old painting of a street urchin levering himself out of a fallen-over wooden box, although Darrell couldn't imagine why he was in there to begin with. The kid's hands grasped the sides of the container, which was also the picture's frame, and one foot stuck up, its toes poking out of the painting as he heaved himself up to make his escape. Or at least, they seemed to. The longer Darrell stared, the more details he marveled at.

Now Darrell knew what he was looking for, spotting links between the donated artwork in the modern and contemporary exhibition halls was easier. He put out his hand to stop loose fifty-dollar bills from fluttering away from the roll that was pinned to a brown panel on the wall, only to feel stupid when that was a trick-the-eye painting too. The jumble of drink cans and snacks, jutting out from the wall and about to fall, didn't fool him after that.

"So let's see the Buckman Room," he suggested. "Buck sure liked tricks and puzzles." And had been generous in donating so much to the museum and city in his later years, although Darrell would have put money on the guy being ruthless when he was younger, getting his business off the ground and making his fortune in a cutthroat field.

"Yes. Seems— Oh, *enigma*!" Aldric stopped halfway down the stairs, and a woman tsked as she nearly banged into him. He colored. "The name of his company. It's enigma, backward!"

Darrell had to chuckle, more so when the Buckman space had a painting taking up one wall of it. As in painted *onto* the wall, its doors, windows and hallway to another room all fake. The shelves and cupboards on it weren't solid, either, or the objects hanging up on it or off it. He nudged Aldric to look at the table at one end of the room, with its pack of cards and mess of papers, ribbons and scissors apparently left lying around on it.

Aldric laughed. "That's a trick painting too, but on a tabletop? Huh, it looks so real, like we could touch the things. I nearly did, that bottle of wine hanging in the straw basket just there. I didn't get at first that it was painted onto the wall."

Darrell checked it out. Yeah, it did look like it was jutting out of the shopping bag and spilling out down the wall. A woman leaped forward, a Kleenex in her hand to wipe up the 'spill', and blushed at having been fooled.

"I guess I should get moving," he said at last. "Not long until my shift."

They reached the door they'd entered when Aldric exclaimed. "I need my keys back. I had to hand them in. Nearly forgot. Won't be a second."

"Sure…" Darrell's attention was taken by a figure out in the garden. Well, two figures. One he knew personally. *Mateo. What is he doing here?* Enjoying the fountain or the abstract sculptures on the lawn, maybe? Darrell didn't know him that well, as it turned out. But the guy with him was someone who Darrell recognized from photos he'd seen recently when looking into the Buckman family. Nick Buckman, Buck's son by his first wife. His estranged son. *Disowned* was one description he'd come across. This was a weird coincidence, and Darrell didn't like coincidences.

"Mateo!" he called, knocking on the glass window then moving to the door. "Over here. It's Darrell." He thought Mateo glanced at him, then turned back to the dark-haired, intense-looking guy with him. Darrell was about to head out to the pair when a cough sounded behind him, and Aldric was there, his gaze directed where Darrell was staring.

"Is everything okay?" he asked.

"What? Yeah." Mateo and Nick had moved, and Darrell couldn't see them through the fountain's spray or the group of people around it. "Yeah. Let's go."

"Okay."

That word again. He'd told Aldric that everything was okay, but he wasn't sure it was.

Chapter Twelve

Aldric had never liked Sundays and hated this one especially, having spent yesterday with Darrell. He'd never liked this crappy studio apartment either, and his time in Darrell's place yesterday had made him dislike this one more. The space and light of that apartment complex filled his mind. Darrell had everything near at hand — open around the clock, probably — whereas Aldric trudged to use the old washing machine in the laundry room of the house the garage apartment belonged to, careful to keep to the times stipulated in his rental agreement.

His next stop was the supermarket. Chores usually filled up a Sunday, but today he wanted time to himself to think about Darrell and sleeping with Darrell. He was sad when the throb in his ass, the reminder of having given himself to Darrell, ceased. His lack of sexual knowledge worried him. Not just the physical stuff, but the etiquette — if there was such a thing. Should he have left after they'd fucked? He had a small feeling Darrell might have preferred that. *Did* prefer that, as a rule. Aldric wished he had the confidence to think *had* preferred that in the past, that things were different now, with him in Darrell's life, but he couldn't. No matter how much he might want to.

Back home again, he lay on the couch and thought some more. He couldn't *think* his way into a relationship with Darrell, but he could try his best to make it happen. Look at how far he'd come. He'd asked Darrell out on a date, and Darrell had accepted. They'd spent the evening together, then the morning together the day after. And between the shared evening and the morning had been…*the night*.

Aldric groaned at his renewed erection. His cock had filled at the most inconvenient times that morning—it seemed so many things reminded him of Darrell. The fresh detergent and fabric softener smell in the laundry room sparked memories of Darrell's bedroom, with its rack of long-sleeved tees and jeans, the polo shirts and pants. The dough and sugar of the pastry counter in the store had brought back the scent and taste of the breakfast Danish Darrell had bought him. The museum program lying on his floor conjured up Darrell in all his crew-cut, broad-shouldered, freckled-nosed glory, his olive-green eyes alight with curiosity as they'd toured the rooms.

Aldric sighed and raised the borrowed Henley to his nose again, inhaling deep. *I'm* in *deep. I got it bad.* His mind raced and plotted, and he didn't dwell on that sexy Latino guy Darrell had called out to in the museum garden, seemingly eager to speak with. *Nope, not going there.* He focused instead on what Darrell would be doing now if they were together…and walked his fingers down his body to his dick as he imagined.

* * * *

Darrell was wondering why his father had asked for his help when he was perfectly capable of laying garden decking all by himself. At least being given the busy work to do meant that Darrell could let his mind chew over the case. It was a serious case now, deserving of more priority than it had gotten — at least, *he* thought so.

Chief had already laid concrete pads on the site he'd squared off prior to Darrell's arrival, so all Darrell had to do was cover the area in a layer of weed-control fabric. Seeing priceless works of art yesterday had made him wonder if some of the artifacts, particularly the puzzle boxes, could be valuable too. The owner and the other guy at the antique store had said those trinkets weren't worth anything to most people, just collectors, and Randa had thought so too, happy to sell them off as a bulk lot. But what if her late husband had mixed one or more valuable ones in with the crap, maybe even on purpose, as a prank, and Randa had realized too late? Were there such things as expensive puzzles or keepsakes? Like ones made of precious gems or gold? Was that what Buck's cast-off son had been doing at the museum, trying to find information about something along those lines?

Darrell's lack of culture or arts knowledge had never bothered him before, but it had since meeting Aldric. He wondered what Aldric was doing today. *Visiting family? Sitting alone in his place, wondering what I'm doing? Touching himself as —*

"Son?"

Darrell startled, then blushed. He ducked his head, hoping to avoid his father's focus. "Yeah. Doing it." He tipped the gravel onto the surface he'd covered and let his thoughts drift back to the case. It was far-reaching, he suspected — or maybe his feelings were. Were his feelings for Aldric, the victim of the initial assault that had started all this, mixing themselves into whatever *this* was? He should keep a closer eye on him. *Pass by the store more often. Ask other cops to.* "Done," he told his father, setting the remaining gravel down. "So, cutting the deck boards, right?" Again, his father could do that.

"Without laying squares of damp-proof course?" Chief raised an incredulous eyebrow.

Excuse me for never having laid a deck in my life. "Planning on entertaining more?" he asked his father, curious as to why he was doing this now. While he couldn't really see his father holding drinks parties in the garden, he could see him relaxing on a lounger there even less.

"The feel of having a bigger usable living space adds to the value of the house. And the garden's not needed now that there are no boys at home," Chief said.

Darrell didn't remember the swing set around the side of the house, although there were photographs of Ryan in it. Chief had replaced it with a jungle gym slash mini assault course as soon as his boys could handle it. "Oh?"

"Thinking of making that kitchen wall into a window wall, too. But the next project's turning your room back into the extra bathroom."

"Turning...back?" He hadn't known his small bedroom had been a bathroom. Travis and Ryan had shared the bigger bedroom, for all Darrell was closer in age to Travis and Ryan was the baby of the family. "Are you selling the place or something?" That could make sense, with Travis now Basic Mission Qualified, and

Ryan probably moving away once he'd finished training.

His father shrugged. "So, son, been busy lately since we had dinner?"

His father didn't do idle chit chat, so his inquiry had Darrell on the alert. "A little, I guess. Why?"

"You called up Leah's friend Brianna yet? Since she saw you having lunch with a guy?"

The one-two punch left Darrell winded. Which was he supposed to react to? *Neither.*

"You remember Leo, from the base? His wife Jean's got family in town and they were showing them around. They saw you at the art museum yesterday."

That Darrell, Chief's son, had been voluntarily partaking of art and culture wasn't exactly the problem, or the reason for the strange note in his father's voice. What was coming next was. Darrell knew it by the frigid ball of fear in his gut.

"With a guy? Was he the same one you were with in the week? You haven't mentioned getting a new partner, so I doubt he's some new cop you were partnered up with. So what's going on, Darrell?"

Darrell didn't need a decoder ring to hear that as, *"What's wrong with you, Darrell? Your brothers are settled down with women, but you…"* There'd be no *"Where did I go wrong?"* from his father. Chief wouldn't countenance that *he* could be at fault. Not that there was any fault or wrongness, because there was nothing wrong with being gay or bi or trans, or anywhere on the rainbow.

Darrell didn't like the way his heart thudded, or the thickening in his throat that prevented him from speaking and saying anything his father didn't want to hear. He also didn't want to have this talk — *the* talk — here, like this. And not just because his father was around heavy tools that could double as weapons. Hell, for Chief, anything could double as a weapon, should he need one.

"Going on?" he hedged. "What do you mean? What are you saying?"

"You've never brought a girl home. Well, not since school." His father had an excellent memory and strove for accuracy. "I accept that the military way of life is not for everyone, sure. Good as it would've been to have three for three boys of mine serving their country."

"To Protect and to Serve." Darrell reminded him of the police force's motto. Would this have been easier over a drink? He'd fucking well get one after. He waited a few seconds for his father to ask outright if he were gay. No, that would be worse, because of the ugly, reductive, shaming synonyms Chief would use for it.

"Is it that you felt unsuitable for serving in the military?" his father asked.

"What, like other people were once felt to be 'unsuitable'?" How long could they dance around this? "You know that the US military was able to adjust, to become more inclusive, first accepting one marginalized group, and…another not that long ago. Or do you wish certain acts, one in particular, weren't repealed?"

His father shocked him by saying, "I don't know."

"I do." Darrell took a couple of steps away. "I know you couldn't accept it. Wouldn't. So maybe the Williams version of Don't Ask, Don't Tell, as applied to so many areas, should just stand." With understanding of just what those areas were. So, business as usual then, with hopefully fewer attempts to fix him up with girls. As bleak and shitty as that was, Darrell could handle it. Had been handling it.

"Accept a son of mine being a faggot?" His father sounded as though someone had said the Navy was the best branch of the armed services, and the others also-rans. "Is that what you're saying to me?"

Darrell sighed and tucked in the flap on the bag of gravel he'd been using, making sure it was neatly put away. The irony of that displacement activity wasn't lost on him. "I'm not saying anything." Neither of them was ready for this, so Darrell switched tracks. Deflected. "I wish I could talk with Mom," he said, half under his breath. "If she were still here."

"Well, she's not." Chief kicked at the planks of wood propped against the wall. "She left, like the quitter she is." He was usually careful not to cram adjectives onto the label he wrapped around the neck of his absent wife and his children's runaway mother, although they hung in the air.

The usual pause that accompanied any mention of his mother filled the space all around them. "Do you ever think stuff could have been handled differently?" That was more than they had ever said on the subject and Darrell was using it as a warm-up. "That you could have handled Mom's problems differently? Any kind of addiction is a disease."

"The *hell*?" Chief stood tall. "You think choosing to get blitzed on vodka is like having *cancer*? So you're saying a woman who doesn't have to go out to work, who lives in a decent house in a good part of the city, who has a husband who doesn't cheat on her, doesn't knock her around and doesn't gamble, is *sick*?"

"I'm saying maybe you could have tried to find out why she needed to drink." He expected his father to take a swing at him over that but pressed on when he didn't. "You just listed a lot of negatives as things she didn't have. That might be a good place to start."

"Don't talk out of your ass, boy," Chief snapped. "Woulda, coulda, shoulda sounds cute—"

"Sung by pansy-asses in a pop song, yeah." At least his father was unlikely to make him chant it in a singsong voice and snap his fingers to accompany it now that he was out of his teens.

"And real men live in reality." Chief delivered the second line in the axiom, as he always had.

Darrell recognized there was no point to this. "Maybe it's best we don't have this talk."

"Or best none of us do anything that could occasion this talk," his father slammed back.

And he'd thought his vision of the rest of his life in relation to his family was bleak. Him avoiding any mention of whatever man he was seeing, or in a relationship with—*yeah, right*—while his brothers married and had kids who fought for Grandpa Jack's approval. His brothers and father managing not to make any reference to him being stag at each and every family event. *Bleak and lonely.*

"I have to go. The patio's looking good. And maybe you should set up a small swing set, where one used to be. Travis and Ashley are sure to be having kids soon."

Because they were in a relationship. Ashley could come to all the family parties and lunches, weave her way into the fabric of the Williams family's life, as could Leah, Ryan's other half. But any guy he dated would be in the shadows, left out of the Brick's Tavern get-togethers, never invited to any celebrations on the base. And who would put up with that? No one in the long-term. So it wasn't fair to even start anything with anyone.

With Aldric. He had to pull back, keep things casual. The next time he spoke to Aldric, he'd make him understand.

*   *   *   *

Monday laughed at Darrell's Sunday plans.

"So, what happened was you had a dream about your late husband" He held the phone away from Randa Buckman's hysterical shout that no, her late husband's *ghost* had appeared.

"And he told you he wants his favorite puzzle box buried with him, and if not, you're—and I quote—'doomed to die an agonizing death'. Is that correct, Mrs. Buckman? I see." He also saw that she wanted him, or any of the SAPD, to pass this along to the antique store for her. How long before she went over Darrell's head on this? She must have contacts higher up in the force. She was gone before he could bid her goodbye, and he hung up.

Sean whistled at what Darrell was writing down and spun his forefinger near his temple. "The death and all the stuff that came with it sent her overboard."

Darrell shrugged, but Sean might have a point. Crazy people did crazy things. And if his suspicions were correct about those artifacts being valuable and a certain party wanting one or more back, it made him worry more about Aldric's safety. *I want everyone safe,* he told himself, but knew he was beginning to care more for Aldric than he should.

"It's me," he said shortly when Aldric answered the phone in the store. The guy didn't even have a cell, in this day and age.

"Hi! How did your visit with your father go?" Aldric replied.

"Don't ask, don't tell. Oh, nothing," he continued, when Aldric made a confused questioning noise. "Look, Randa called."

He filled Aldric in on developments and his theories, wondering if he should be telling this to Elliot instead.

"Jonas has been researching the symbols left and doesn't think they're connected to cults or curses," Aldric said. "And from what I've been studying too, it can't be a case of the artifact being really valuable and sold by mistake. That can't be why Randa wants it back. The puzzle boxes are nice and interesting, but there's never been any made that are worth any money, and there's nothing valuable in the Buckman items."

"So what's your explanation?"

"I don't know." Darrell could imagine him shrugging those round shoulders. "Some cruel joke on Randa? Maybe someone Buck bested or ruined in business getting revenge on his wife? Or someone from her life or past playing about? I have to go."

Darrell didn't suggest another meeting — although he wanted to — just said goodbye instead. He busied himself in work straightaway, checking up on Nick Buckman. As he'd thought, the guy was not exactly an upstanding citizen, and it was interesting that he was now back in SA after questionable business dealings out of state. From police reports, the guy was no stranger to threatening or lying to get what he wanted. *Fuck.*

Mateo didn't pick up when Darrell called. Once the voicemail kicked in, Darrell left his message. "You know who this is, just as I know you saw me on

Sunday. Listen, I don't give a crap about any stupid antiques you or anyone might want, or if you or anyone are trying to piss off Randa Buckman. But don't involve Aldric or you'll be fucking sorry. Got that?"

The more he thought about it, the more he was convinced Nick Buckman was trying to scare his stepmother into handing him some share of the estate, and Aldric had gotten caught in the crossfire.

He managed to get a little free time that afternoon to talk to Aldric in person and let him know his thoughts.

Sean dropped him there and drove off, leaving Darrell on the sidewalk outside the store. One look through the window at Aldric's pale, stricken face, and Darrell was charging inside, his hand going for his weapon, his anxious voice demanding, "What's wrong? What's happened?"

Chapter Thirteen

"Aldric?" Darrell pressed. "Are you alone?"

His question took a few seconds to sink in. Aldric glanced around the store. Yes, just him, alone, no customers or staff, and standing behind the counter with his hand on Elliot's old-fashioned landline phone. He nodded. "Jonas doesn't work today, and Elliot's at a client's, discussing an acquisition that he or she wants."

Darrell holstered his gun. "And did something happen?"

"A phone call." Only just realizing now he was still touching the phone, Aldric dropped his hand.

"From...?"

"I don't know. Anonymous!" Aldric shook his head, like a dog coming out of water.

"Sit down." Darrell helped Aldric walk the few steps to the chair behind the counter and his hand on Aldric's shoulder had Aldric bending at the knees to drop into it.

"Where can I get some water?" Darrell asked, and Aldric wondered if that was worry or irritation he heard in Darrell's voice.

"Oh. There." Aldric pointed to the table he now knew to be saber legged, which meant the legs flared out like curved swords. It held the tea-making equipment that he still associated with his first day here — even though Elliot made the fragrant brew twice a day, before lunch and before dinner — and also a glass jug filled with water. The glasses set out around it didn't match it or one another. "Thank you. I'm fine." Darrell saw him when he was overwhelmed too often, for one reason or another.

"What did the person on the phone want?" Darrell kept his voice light, as if the matter were nothing, and seemed more focused on handing Aldric a paper napkin.

"They — he, I think — said to bring Buck's favorite Japanese puzzle box and hand it over if I value my life." His teeth chattered as he said the last part. He felt stupid for being so upset, but the call, the rough, disguised voice, was just registering with him, as well as the words that had been spoken. He slid off his glasses and polished them with the napkin.

"Hey." Darrell slipped behind him and rubbed his back. "It's okay."

Aldric twisted to see him. "It's a prank, a cruel joke, like we said, right?"

Darrell brushed a soft kiss across his cheek. "Did it sound like a prank?"

Aldric shook his head. "N-no. It was…it was scary."

"Do you know which box they meant? Which was his favorite?" Darrell continued in his soothing voice, and Aldric could just see him interviewing people like that, dealing with them in that reassuring way. A far cry from how he'd interacted with Aldric at their first meeting. The difference almost made Aldric snort.

"I do now. The caller described it. Hexagonal with white inlays. There are a couple of hexagonal ones, and a few have pale inlays or applique bits on, but only one box fits the description. Huh. Like those diagrams you learn in math." He drew circles with both forefingers.

"Venn diagram." Darrell said it as though he understood what Aldric was talking about, what he was seeing in his mind's eye. "And take it where and when?"

"The Spanish Mission in two hours' time." Aldric waved a hand in the direction he thought the missions lay, in San Antonio Missions National Historical Park. "The San Jose Mission," he added before Darrell could ask which one in that calm voice that didn't make questions seem like an interrogation.

It occurred to him that this was probably a police matter. Well, Officer Williams was here. And, *damn*, Darrell looked good in his uniform. When Aldric thought about him, which was a lot, he pictured him in that, not in jeans or slacks. Aldric's mind also dwelt on Darrell's nightstick, and his handcuffs. He raised his eyes to Darrell's face, seeing the tightness there and the clench to his jaw.

"You're angry with me?" The question slipped out before Aldric could put a brake on it.

"What? No, not *with* you — because of what's happened to you!" burst from Darrell. "I'm furious that call scared you, babe. And I'm angry with whoever made it. When I catch them —" He grimaced and shook his head.

Aldric passed him the glass of water, and Darrel's well-shaped lips kicked up a little on one side before he drank. Aldric was scared, yeah, and despite his efforts, he hadn't done a good job of hiding it. That Darrell was angry for him and concerned about him thrilled him. He took the glass back from Darrell just so he could touch his hand. When, after he'd set the glass down, Darrell caught his hand and held it, it felt as though he'd won a prize. *Run a marathon. Run a race then won a medal.*

"Elliot told me to close up and not be here alone," he said, thinking of his boss' concern.

"Oh?" Darrell's voice sharpened, his eyes narrowing.

It must be his cop antennae twitching.

"Is he jumpy? Nervous?" Darrell prodded. "Or acting different?"

Aldric frowned, thinking. "I don't know. No. he's just caring. Protective, I suppose you'd call it. He's—"

The bells tinkled, signaling that the door was opening. Darrell shoved himself in front of Aldric and placed one hand on his holstered weapon.

"Aldric?" Meredith's voice was higher than usual and she sounded confused.

"It's Meredith, from the restaurant over the road," he hissed at Darrell, bobbing his head around Darrell's body so their neighbor could see him—as difficult as that was when he'd gone rigid with nerves. He pushed to his feet then brushed against Darrell and felt the taut thrum of tension in him too.

"Is everything okay? Not more vandalism, or, God, not another attack?" she questioned, her gaze on Darrell.

"No. Officer Williams is just checking in," Aldric answered. "Did you want something, Meredith?"

"Erm, yeah. Elliot usually gets a dinner today and the boss wanted to check on him since he hasn't called his order in."

"He thought he might be delayed, but he mentioned he'd be back here later, so he'll want dinner," Aldric guessed. Elliot ordered from Cabot's Brasserie at least twice a week and insisted Aldric and Jonas join him as his guests if they happened to be around.

"Well, let's hope he's back before we close!" Meredith knocked on the wood of a cabinet near her then left.

Darrell took a few steps around the store, and Aldric studied his back view. Darrell was not an over-muscled jock, and wasn't even particularly tall, although he was strong, his body buff. Aldric liked him the way he was. He followed him and stroked a hand down Darrell's back. It was as toned as he remembered. *Fantasized about.*

"Careful." Darrell jerked away, his gaze on the store's glass windows.

Aldric hoped Darrell wasn't doing what he thought he was and decided to test his suspicions. "Are we going back to the drive-in for our next date? If we wanted to go for a meal out, the restaurant across there is really good. Oh, you probably know it, as you live near here, right?"

"Aldric." Darrell twisted over his shoulder to glance at him. "Not now." He turned back to the door when the bells sounded, and it opened again. "Sean. Officer O'Hara."

"Thought you were only gonna be a minute?" Darrell's partner said. He came in, studying Darrell. "What?"

"Shut the door and turn the key." Darrell raised his chin at it, then crossed to the window to pull the blinds down.

"What's up?" Sean looked at Aldric. "Developments?"

"Can we talk in that office in the back?"

It wasn't a question, not when Darrell was leading the way as he spoke. Aldric hadn't been able to appreciate seeing Darrell as a patrol officer the night they'd met and had tried to imagine him working at the station, or out on the beat, like something from a TV show. But now, with him filling in his partner— this was how he'd envisioned Darrell on the job.

"A puzzle box?" Sean reared back in his chair when Darrell reached that part of the story. "Like in *Hellraiser*?"

"What?" Aldric didn't understand, but saw Darrell fighting a smile.

"Movie," he replied. "Maybe. You'll get used to Sean, Aldric. He's…imaginative."

Sean's forehead creased. "So you two are friends, now? While working on this?"

"Sean, listen." Darrell glanced at him and swiped a hand over his mouth. "I haven't called this in."

Sean frowned. "Because you still think it's a prank? On who? Both the widow and this store? Or maybe it's revenge?"

Darrell flinched a little at that, and Aldric wondered why.

135

"But seems to me we're back to robbery." Sean scratched his red head. "Is this particular box valuable?"

"No. It's modern, and even the older ones were common. They were used as decorative jewelry cases. Look." Aldric reached for the guide to the trinkets he'd been studying. "They're just carved wood, some of it in mosaic patterns. I showed you before. In the safe, when you were checking that it was secure."

"I can't recall." Darrell didn't meet his eyes. "And they're not here now?"

"They are. Elliot hasn't taken them to the depository yet. Do you want to see them?" He directed that at Sean, who was looking uncomfortable. Not waiting for a reply, Aldric led the way to the small, secure room next door to the office that served as the premises' walk-in safe then keyed in the code to open it.

Inside, he took up the hexagonal box. "This one must be the one in question." He pressed some of the pearl inlay squares.

"Don't open it!" Sean ordered, his eyes wide and his hands out as if to brace for an explosion.

"I can't. I don't know all the moves. I've only managed to open this simple rectangular one, and that was done by pure luck," Aldric admitted. "Lots of times, if you do make the mechanism work, you don't know you did it, so you lock it again."

"This one's similar." Darrell picked up a five-sided box.

"Why would you want a similar... Fuck, Dazzle! Sorry, Aldric." Sean grabbed Darrell's arm. "Tell me you want a decoy box to take to Fuentes and let him handle this."

"*This*?" Aldric asked.

Sean nodded. "I know my partner. He's planning something crazy because Fuentes has been as useless as tits on a boar hog."

Darrell snorted but didn't speak.

"Like a trap?" Aldric's mind raced as Darrell followed Sean out of the small room, arguing and persuading his partner that they should be the ones to hand the artifact over, not Aldric. Aldric locked the safe, catching references to Sean being similar in build, to a recent operation they'd pulled off and how well they worked as a team.

"We'd need to study the drop zone and we'd need backup stationed at three points," Sean protested. "How is that gonna happen when Fuentes is ignoring this whole thing?"

"Here." Darrell freed an old map from a rack on the wall. "You can pull up a map on your cell too and so can I." He took out his phone.

"We're in uniform," Sean pointed out.

"We got clothes in the car. Come on."

Aldric still didn't understand when they left the store, promising to be back within minutes. He heard a buzzing noise. Darrell's phone, left on the table, was ringing. A handsome face filled the screen. The guy Darrell had been trying to talk to at the museum. *Mateo*, it said. The door opened and the two men were back.

"Darrell." Aldric indicated his phone, needing to ask about the call. *About Mateo.*

"Thanks." Darrell slipped it into his pocket. "Right. We'll change and go," he announced.

"But…okay." Aldric, confused, forced himself to switch tracks. "It's the end of my hours, anyway." And he could find a way to ask about the phone call on the journey.

"No. Not you. You're staying here."

Sean pulled a baseball cap low on his head. "A decoy box and a decoy courier. I dunno how you talked me into this." He vanished into the back.

"I'm not going? But—" Aldric was still protesting when the police officers set off…which was when his stubborn streak set in.

Darrell thinks I'm weak and feeble, does he? His final words had been to keep out of sight, to stay safe. So he was supposed to hide behind closed doors, while Darrell had…adventures. *Like with that Mateo guy.* Well, Aldric would show him. He grabbed his jacket and keys, making sure the store's van keys were among them, then locked up, intent on following Darrell.

Chapter Fourteen

Darrell looked at Sean out of the corners of his eyes as they walked. "Could you try to look less like a cop and more like Aldric?"

"I am a cop, and I don't know that dude very well." Sean slowed and glanced around. They'd left the car at the very end of the visitors' center parking lot and were trekking the long way to the church at the back of the mission, going through the lot and past the welcome point, as if they were ordinary sightseers.

"Queen of the Missions. And second place I've been in a week that I went to on field trips," Darrell said, hoping his conversation would deflect any lob before Sean served it. He didn't want to have anything even *approaching* the conversation he could sense was looming on the horizon. Sure, Sean was his partner, even his buddy. But the risk of him reacting negatively to Darrell announcing *yeah, I'm gay* was too big to take.

"Do you? Know the guy that well?" Sean prodded.

"A little." Darrell checked his watch. They should speed up a bit, without seeming to hurry. "There's the bastion." He pointed to the ball of the tower-like part projecting from the fort's corner. "Did you pronounce it 'bastard' when you came here as a kid?"

"Huh? Why are you changing the subject?"

"I'm not." He was trying to. "Just making a dumb joke. We grabbed lunch the other day." Was that enough of a bone to throw? *Ooh.* Unfortunate choice of word—it was too close to boner, something *Darrell* was too close to, thinking about the other meals he'd grabbed with...and from...Aldric.

"I'm not stupid. I figured out...stuff about you." Sean nudged him. "Like why we don't see you with chicks."

Darrell's heart sank. "I don't get why you're asking me about this now. And I don't expect you to understand."

"Asking you now because you're, I don't know, *different*, somehow, now, okay?" Sean didn't sound angry. He sounded almost like they were having one of their regular conversations about stuff.

"Am I?" Darrell wondered out loud. Aldric had gotten under his skin. Into his blood, maybe. Did that show? If it did, how did Darrell feel about it? He'd avoided commitment for so long, but now he thought he might want it—with Aldric.

Sean nudged him again, harder. "And I might understand if you fucking explained it to me, *partner.*"

Which was more of a concession than he'd ever imagined getting. "I'd have to understand it myself first." He sighed. "Maybe I could try talking about it, over a beer?"

"If you're buying." It was Sean's standard reply. God alone knew what he spent his money on.

"How about over a game of pool? At which I will beat you," Darrell promised.

"Those tables in your fancy residential complex are shit. The floor slants, or something." This reply of Sean's was automatic too. He hated to lose. "I choose the place, okay?"

"I'll still win." No one could out-trash-talk Darrell, or any kid who'd grown up in his family. "And thanks."

Sean's upraised finger told him he was verging on 'feelings and crap' ground. "Better focus up here."

The place was almost closing — the guide stationed just inside the walls by the Native American quarters was trying to convince stragglers to leave the vast square, and it took them flashing their badges and Sean turning his persuasive charm on the woman to get them in.

It was creepy, the trees seeming to absorb the light, and yet the grass looked too bright a green for the gray-brown buildings and pathways. The old limestone looked like it might crumble, and the stones, all different sizes and shapes, might pop themselves free of their cement — or whatever it was that held them together — and tumble down on them.

The church was on the far side of the mission, and as Darrell walked beside Sean, a bell tolled, the sound mournful in the late-afternoon air.

"Fuck." Sean's hand jerked as if he wanted to cross himself and he scowled. "Better not be any weird-ass time-slip shit going on," he warned Darrell, as though Darrell had been plotting just that and would now drop the idea.

He knew where Sean was coming from. The gaping arches of the colonnades surrounding the church seemed to be lying in wait for them, to lure them into dead-end courtyards like a labyrinth. The hollowed-out rectangles and squares cut into the walls caught Darrell's eye. They weren't old doors or windows — some looked like hatches, except they didn't go through to anywhere, and he tried to remember what the people who'd built the missions had once placed in them. A semicircle at the bottom of a wall had been for a fire. He could tell from the blackened state of the stone, and the chimney, complete with vents, built into the wall.

The empty doorways and windows in the walls added a desolate air to the building, but coming across barred ones was worse. Darrell was relatively glad to push the huge brown door to the church open, although he jumped when it was pulled from his hands — a couple were coming out as he and Sean tried to enter. He almost gasped at the richness and brightness of the church after the emptiness of outside. Well, the altar, anyway. Its blue and gold made the place seem bright, like the white of the walls and the high ceiling made the long, narrow building seem bigger.

"There, right?" Sean swung a foot at the first polished dark-wood bench of seats before the platform at the front. "Leave it there?"

"Yeah." He kept watch as Sean placed the bag with the dummy box in it at the end of the bench.

Sean came back and jerked his head to the right. "Someone's there, on the other side. A few rows back. Crouched down."

"Praying." Darrell had spotted the elderly woman kneeling on the floor between her seat and the one in front.

"You think that's—"

"No. Hey, pew-pew!"

"What?"

"The benches are called pews and when we were kids, if we were taken into a church, we used to pretend to shoot and go 'pew-pew'." It didn't sound funny now that Darrell mentioned it.

"Heathen." Sean didn't seem to find it amusing either. "That why you became a cop?"

Darrell shrugged. It was as probable as any other reason. The woman stood and inched her way out of the pew to walk to the front of the building. She gave them a hard stare as she passed them to exit. "We should make ourselves scarce," he suggested.

"Move away from the bag," Sean mocked. "I still think this is some stupid trick. A classic would be getting someone here to do this, then robbing their place."

"Maybe." Darrell led the way down the central aisle to the back of the church. He squeezed down a pew to look at the small plaque on the wall. There wasn't a great deal to see. "If this was a Dan Brown book, there'd be clues in the paintings on the wall, or even up there, in those designs on the ceiling," he said.

"And I'd get to fuck the snobby foreign chick with a stick up her ass," Sean replied. "She'd be, like, a history professor or nuclear physicist or something, with those little black glasses, but wearing really high heels."

"Which never seem to stop the women when they have to run their asses off to the next location," Darrell pointed out.

"Oh, and she's a martial arts expert. Tries to take me down, but I'm better," Sean proclaimed. "That's when her hair escapes from the clip or bun or whatever the fuck it's called."

Darrell eyed him. "You really put thought into this, huh?" It would definitely be more exciting than this, trying to kill time and remain unobtrusive, while keeping a watch on a package thirty feet away.

Thirty minutes in, Sean was the first to crack. "Nothing's happening. This is whack."

"Let's check out the front of the church," Darrell suggested.

Sean's face showed what he thought of defiling the altar. Their bag was still there, still in the position they'd left it. Darrell noticed a door to the left of the entrance, and checking all around, pushed it open. He peered into the small anteroom it led to. "What's this for?" he asked Sean.

"The hell should I know? Oh, Jesus. Damn. Sorry!" Sean apologized to the room in general. "Bathroom?"

It wasn't. It was just a storeroom, or changing room or waiting room. Darrell resisted making a 'three-in-one, just like the trinity' crack. Suddenly the door they'd come in through was pushed open and a portly man in black clothes came in and froze, his wide eyes and flared nostrils suggesting he was startled to see them there.

"You shouldn't be in here. Who are you?" he demanded.

Startled and angry. "SAPD." Darrell took out his badge.

"And?" the man continued, advancing.

"And who are you?" Sean O'Hara, king of the comebacks.

"The deacon, for *your* information." The man accompanied this with a finger pointed in Sean's chest. "The mission is closed to the public at this time."

"Yes—" Darrell started.

"And the police hold no jurisdiction in a church."

"We—" Sean tried.

"Well?" cried the man, rounding on them both. "What have you got to say for yourselves?"

"That we're just leaving," Darrell answered, nudging his shoulder into Sean's to slide him away. He grabbed the bag from the pew before they made a hasty retreat.

"Lovely church you have here, Deacon," Sean said as they exited.

"You do know that sounded exactly like you were gonna add 'shame if something happened to it'?" Darrell said.

"This was fucking stupid, Dazzle!" Sean burst out. "And not just a waste of time and manpower, which we'll have to account for, officially or unofficially, back at the station. I mean if that idiot calls Fuentes, we could be screwed."

"You play hunches all the time," Darrell protested, jogging to keep up with his partner.

Sean cast him an angry look. "Yeah, but not because I'm trying to get in someone's pants."

"Yeah you do!" They were sprinting through the grassy garden now, heading back the way they'd come, then through the gate in the wall.

"Well, I don't wanna get in trouble over some guy who's—" Sean almost tripped as he came to a sudden stop. "Here."

Darrell just managed to keep from slamming into his partner as he frowned at Sean. "Who's —" Then he saw him, and Darrell's lungs seized with fear. "Aldric?"

Sean was right. Aldric was there, on the path that led from the mission to the visitor center.

"I thought I told you not to be here," Darrell grated at Aldric, his anger at Sean finding an outlet.

"I can go where I like." Aldric sounded as pissed as Sean, who scoffed.

"You were right," he said to Darrell, making him frown in response. "When you said you didn't expect me to understand." Sean sighed. "Look, see you at the station, yeah? Where we'd better hope we can fix this." Sean gave them both a curt nod and left.

"It didn't seem too dangerous, or whatever reason it was for you telling me to stay behind. Not if no one came for the box." Aldric took the bag from Darrell.

He'd put it in an Intrinsic Value bag, Darrell noticed, when Aldric shook it out by the handles. Darrell had been carrying it folded over, to hold it more securely. Aldric's words stung, just as Sean's had. "You're sure it was in the church? And this mission?"

"Yes. I'm not stupid." Aldric looked as though he might stamp a foot. "I would have been here sooner, but Randa Buckman called."

"She did? What did she want?"

"She was almost hysterical, begging the store to at least let her see her husband's prized possessions once more. I replied I couldn't say yes or no because I was only an employee."

"Wait." Darrell's brain was spinning, his mouth struggling to catch up. "An employee who wasn't supposed to be at the store at that time, because he should have been a few miles away, in response to a phone call. Of course no one showed up, if someone was listening and knew the handover was a setup!"

"So this is my fault?" Aldric demanded, his cheeks darkening with a blush.

Before Darrell could answer Aldric's question, his cell rang, and he took it out on reflex. He tried to silence it but answered it by mistake. "Mateo? Not now. Really bad time. No. Wait. I need to talk to you." He remembered his suspicions. Was it a coincidence that Mateo, who was probably working with the guy Darrell suspected was behind this, was calling now? "Hey, where are you going?"

The last was to Aldric, who'd turned and stalked off down the path leading to Roosevelt Avenue, the plastic bag swinging from his wrist which was jammed through the handles. Cursing, Darrell looked down at his cell phone, to see if Mateo was still there. He wasn't—the call had disconnected. Should he call back?

A shriek made him look up, and his heart squeezed to a stop. "No!" he yelled, uselessly. "*Shit!*"

Aldric was fighting off two men who'd grabbed him and were dragging him toward the avenue. The avenue, where traffic flowed, making pursuit difficult, and where several parked cars, one of which was probably theirs, waited—making escape easy.

"*Aldric!*" Darrell started running. Fast.

Chapter Fifteen

"Get your hands off me! What do you think you're doing?" Aldric cried to the figures dressed in black who'd rushed out from behind the half-wall of the mission building to one side of the path and surrounded him. Well, he tried to yell, but only got out a few words before the guy behind him wrapped an arm around his windpipe, cutting him off.

Who the hell are these men? He *assumed* they were men by their build, but their black hoodies, with the hoods up, made it hard to tell. He struggled then stumbled as he was pushed and pulled along. The one in front of him twisted round, grabbing at the plastic bag Aldric had dangling from his wrist. Aldric, feeling stupid, only then made the connection.

Darrell and Officer O'Hara had come here to pretend to give the fake artifact to whoever was after it, with their plan being to capture the person responsible. And instead Aldric was the one *really* getting taken away.

The road was right in front of him. He'd left his vehicle there. Had these crooks done the same? And if they succeeded in getting him inside their car, he'd be in grave danger.

"Freeze! Police officer!"

Darrell!

"I am armed and will shoot. Repeat. SAPD officer prepared to open fire!" Darrell called out with steel in his voice. "Stop, now!"

That had the men halting in their tracks for a second or two, then continuing, but more jerkily, zigzagging, Aldric almost tripping and falling with each lunging step. He thought he could work out why. A police officer was less likely to shoot if an innocent party was in the way. That was the reason criminals took civilian hostages. Aldric didn't watch many thrillers or action movies, but movies he tended to like had one thing in common. The heroine didn't wait around for a man to rescue her. She rescued herself.

With as much force as he could manage, Aldric rammed his head back to hit the face of the man holding him. In an ideal world, it would break his captor's nose, but he'd take what he could get. At the same time, he brought his heel down as hard as he could on the top of the man's foot. The man swore and loosened his hold, and before he could tighten it again, Aldric wrenched himself away from him and the other guy.

The plastic bag he was carrying and that the man was tearing at ripped in the struggle, the handles staying with Aldric and the body of the bag falling to the ground. Aldric had no time to think about that, however — not when he was close enough to the man who'd been holding him. He spun and kneed him in the balls as hard as he could. It worked. With a cry like an animal, the guy bent over, curling into himself.

The amount of force Aldric had put into the maneuver had him staggering sideways, and he put his foot down awkwardly, at an odd angle. It sent him crashing to the ground. His hands flew out to break his fall, but he still ended up with a face full of gravel.

"Aldric! Are you okay?" Darrell demanded, appearing beside him.

Aldric nodded, groping for his lost glasses. Darrell clapped him on the shoulder then raced off after the crooks. Well, just the one who had been slowed down by Aldric's assault on his balls. Panting, coughing, Aldric had got to his knees when he saw Darrell leap on top of the guy. Aldric cried out, because he could see what Darrell probably couldn't, from his low, flat position—the other, faster guy whirled around and sprinted back to the two figures on the ground.

"*Darrell!*" yelled Aldric, intending to warn him. And oh God, he wished he hadn't when Darrell levered half-off the guy he'd tackled to look back at him, giving the second man the opening he needed to kick out at Darrell. Aldric couldn't see where the kick connected, but it sent Darrell sprawling backward. Another kick, this time to his stomach, kept him there long enough for the guy to scoop his accomplice up and drag him along the remaining section of the path to a silver car. They were gone in seconds, pulling out into the traffic along Roosevelt Avenue in a blare of car horns.

"*Darrell!*" He was already on his feet and holding his side when Aldric reached him.

"Damn. They got away, and I didn't get the license plate," he said. "Did you see anything that would identify them?"

Aldric ignored that. "Darrell, you're *hurt*."

"I'm okay." Darrell shook his head. "Bastard got in a lucky blow. Got my rib."

"Oh no!" Aldric coughed a little to get his voice working properly. "Do you need to go to the hospital? Of course you do. X-rays and machines that beep."

"No." Darrell's hand cut him off. "Ribs heal. It's probably just bruised. Ice, painkillers, I'll be fine. What about you?"

"I have those things. At home. In my apartment. Come on." He took Darrell's arm.

"'S that?" Darrell felt the lump on Aldric's chest and started to laugh, clutching his side. "You still got the puzzle box?"

"Yes, of course." Aldric produced it from under his jacket where he'd shoved it after snatching it up from the ground. "It's Intrinsic Value stock, and I have to return it."

Darrell was still chuckling when they reached the small van with the name of the store on the side. "You came in this? I thought you didn't drive?"

"I don't as in I don't have a car. I do as in I can." Aldric's attention was focused on the road, the traffic and pulling out into it. He pretended not to hear Darrel's muttered, "You can't," or see how he clung to the Jesus strap, his knuckles white. Okay, so he rarely got behind a wheel and needed practice.

"But you're okay?" Darrell asked again. "You hit the ground pretty hard."

"I hit that creep harder though." Aldric grinned.

"Yeah, you did. Nice moves." Darrell smiled back at him. "Did you take self-defense classes?"

"I watch YouTube videos." He wasn't going to say which lady instructor's clips he liked to watch, or more accurately, listen to when he went to sleep. Some of it must have stuck. He'd leave her a comment.

When they reached his garage apartment, he got out first to open the passenger-side door and made sure he walked up the stairs behind Darrell, in case he stumbled. Darrell was taking slow, deep breaths. "There's a first-aid box in the bathroom. Come on." Aldric went to lead the way.

"I can do it."

Aldric stared after Darrell as he walked off. Sure, he liked to see his tight butt and strong thighs, but he was wondering if he'd upset him. He'd only offered to help. *Ice.* He'd promised ice. *Water.* Darrell would need some. He drank a glass himself and had another poured when Darrell came out. "Did you find the ibuprofen?"

Darrell showed him the orange tablets in his hand that he swallowed with the water. "Thanks. My ribs aren't broken. There's a little swelling, but I didn't hear a crack and I would be in a lot more pain."

Aldric's eyes stung with tears he refused to shed. "I'm so sorry. If it wasn't for me, you wouldn't have gotten hurt."

"Call this hurt?" Darrell stripped off his long-sleeved tee and twisted a little to show Aldric the redness on his upper chest that spread to his side. Aldric should have been concerned, but when he reached out to touch, his fingers soon left the bruising spot and crept up to Darrell's nipples. When he reached them, he feathered a thumb over one.

Darrell's face cracked into a grin. "I thought you were going to hold an ice pack to me. But maybe I should check you're not hurt. A thorough examination?"

"How? I mean yes." He couldn't stop toying with Darrell's nipple, now drawing his thumbnail across it. Darrell shivered.

"Maybe here's not the best place."

Aldric knew that. He was under no illusions that his apartment was conducive to spontaneous sex in the living room. There was no wide, inviting couch and the carpet was threadbare. He dropped his hand.

"So, the bedroom?" Darrell prompted, curling his hand around Aldric's hip, then cupping his ass on the way.

This is better, Darrell thought, taking the lead again. His ribs were tender and would be sore for days, but he was fine. He'd power through. He'd done so through worse. Darrell didn't need someone worrying over him and taking care of him—*babying me*. Aldric was *his* babe, not the other way around. It was fine for Aldric—timid, fluffy-haired Aldric—to be hesitant and unsure, needing support and guidance, reassurance and softness, but not him.

Inside Aldric's small bedroom, Darrell made a quick scan of the contents, glad there was a double bed. And Aldric had mentioned a patio, which, from the position of the building, must face the small park over the back. *Hmm.* Privacy outdoors could be fun. He switched off the overhead light and turned on the small lamp next to the bed, pleased with the intimate glow it gave off.

"C'mere, gorgeous," he ordered, pulling Aldric in to nuzzle his neck, then trailing his lips over his jawline before laying a long, deep kiss on him. "Wanna see a really sexy man?" He turned Aldric to face the long strip of mirror propped against the wall.

A pretty pink blush spread over Aldric's face. His eyes were huge and luminous in the mirror's reflection. "W-what are you doing?"

"Showing you." He reached around Aldric to unbutton his shirt. Darrell pushed it open, then caressed his chest. "Nice," he whispered into Aldric's ear, seeing his knees buckle. "Ever considered a piercing?" He pinched both nipples hard between forefingers and thumbs as he spoke.

Aldric moaned, a long, low sound of need. He panted for a moment before answering. "There was a guy in high school. Had a nipple ring in one and a bar in the other. He was a rebel. I liked the look. Wanted..."

"His style or him?" Darrell asked. Close to Aldric, he felt more than saw the shrug he gave and squeezed his nipples to go along with it.

"Both." Aldric gasped but gave no sign that he wanted Darrell to stop.

Interesting. Darrell tugged then twisted. "And?"

Aldric shuddered from head to toe. "Oh...oh...that feels so...mmmm."

"The guy?" Darrell asked, enjoying the way his lover was unraveling. "Tell me."

Aldric gulped and took a shaky breath. "I tried, but it didn't work out."

His fingers still tormenting Aldric's swelling nubs of flesh, Darrell could tell Aldric didn't mean he'd tried a homemade piercing. "With the guy."

"For prom."

"Ooh." Darrell winced for Aldric. He'd get the full story later, although he could guess that it had gone so badly that Aldric hadn't tried or maybe hadn't *dared* to date guys again. At the moment, he had other things to do. He smoothed his hands down to unbutton Aldric's fly and unzip his pants, smiling when he felt Aldric's growing hardness under his palm. "His loss. My gain," he assured Aldric. And he meant it.

He let Aldric's cock spring free, wrapping his hand around the stiff flesh. "You've got a nice size dick on you. It filled my mouth well." He'd deduced before that Aldric liked dirty talk. Pre-cum was already slicking the head of his cock, making it easier to work him. "You liked me blowing you, huh?" Aldric's frantic nod nearly smacked his head into Darrell's forehead, like he'd done to the creep earlier. "Taking you deep, feeling you thrusting in my throat, got me hard. One day soon, I'd love you to really fuck my face. Hold my head and just fuck me until you scream and come down my throat."

Aldric's guttural moan filled the small room.

"Wanna see what you look like with your dick down my throat?" Darrell continued, relentless, indicating the mirror. Before Aldric could stammer out a reply, Darrell was on his knees in front of him, sliding his lips from the tip of his shaft to the base in a smooth, practiced glide that tore a moan from deep inside Aldric. He pulsed in Darrell's mouth and more pre-cum leak from his slit, the taste making Darrell's cock as hard as his nightstick.

"No. Stop." Aldric shifted his hips and pulled free. "You—you're always doing that. I want to. To you." He heaved in a breath. "I want to suck your cock. Please."

Chapter Sixteen

Darrell had never had anybody beg to suck him off before. To have Aldric do so now turned him on unbearably. "Undress me," he said, moving so Aldric had room. Aldric's eyes went wide, and his fingers fumbled a little as he took Darrell up on his invitation, but he got the first couple of fly buttons to his fly undone.

"Not used to these," he confessed, tugging at the lower ones.

"It's easier without a huge erection in the way," Darrell agreed. "But then, that's your fault. And we're stuck in a loop here. The more you get your hands on me there, the more I'm raring to go, giving you less room to work."

"Sorry!" Aldric yanked a little hard, rocking Darrell on his feet.

"It all adds to the anticipation." Darrell believed that about button-fly over zippered jeans. He liked being able to open all five buttons in one quick and satisfying series of pops when speed was of the essence, and also drawing it out to tease a partner by popping one at a time. Now, though, with his dick grateful for each slow centimeter of freedom Aldric gave it, Darrell feared he'd come sooner than he wanted to. *Think about Fuentes. And Miller. Ugh. That helped.* It almost helped too much. Still, it did the job, pushing back his urge to come in minutes.

"Let me do the rest." He toed off his shoes and socks then shoved his pants and briefs off as well.

"You're just right." Aldric tipped his head to one side, like he had in the museum. "All those muscles, but they're not too big and bulky."

"Thanks." Darrell stripped Aldric, leaving his glasses on his naked body. *Jesus*, Darrell found that sexy. He gave him a gentle push onto the bed before he could cross his arms around himself or cover his groin. "You've got nothing to hide either." Darrell positioned Aldric on his back and eased down the bed.

Aldric's face creased. "But I wanted —"

"In a minute. I want to taste you some more." Darrell pushed him flat when he tried to sit up and stroked Aldric's soft, pale inner thighs, feeling the skin quiver and pebble under his fingertips. The crease where leg became hip had always been a favorite body part for Darrell and he feathered along Aldric's now, enjoying the gasps escaping from Aldric's lips in response.

Darrell bent low to trace his tongue down the path that his fingers had forged, and Aldric's dick jerked. A pearl of pre-cum leaked from Aldric's slit. "Gotta clean that up," Darrell murmured. He licked Aldric's cockhead clean, slowly scooping into the slit with the tip of his tongue.

"You tasted there already," Aldric whined when Darrell tongued the vein he'd investigated before, now following it home to the base of Aldric's shaft.

"Okay, fine. But not here I didn't." Darrell's reply came out muffled when he nosed into Aldric's balls. He sucked one into his mouth and Aldric's hips jerked off the bed in an almost violent reflex. "Because I want you in my mouth as well, we're gonna have to do something we haven't yet." He made quick eye contact with Aldric as notice of what he intended to start next, and Aldric biting into his lower lip had Darrell's cock jumping in response. "Don't do anything you don't feel like, okay? And if you try something and it doesn't feel good to you, stop. Same as you'd tell me to stop if I do anything you're not enjoying."

He waited for Aldric's nod before lying on his side next to him, but the wrong way around. Or the right way for what he had in mind. His cock was level with Aldric's mouth, but Darrell wanted Aldric to find his own way to it. There was no rush. He had plenty to play with—*plenty* being a good name for Aldric's dick, which had a nice, thick girth Darrell was swirling his tongue around.

Aldric's curiosity won out over any nervousness he might have had quicker than Darrell had imagined it would. The tentative wet swipe to Darrell's tip was a thrill, knowing he was the first that Aldric had done this to. *Or am I?* Darrell had made a couple of assumptions about the timid, naïve guy before, only to discover they were wrong. And just because he'd never had anal sex didn't mean he hadn't given head. He tried to assess whether the laps of Aldric's tongue spoke of experience.

Aldric's ministrations earned him a spurt of pre-cum, and Darrell wondered how he'd deal with that. A second later, Aldric swallowed. Well, that answered that, and it made Darrell throb harder. He hoped Aldric could take his thickening-by-the-second cock. Within a minute, it was clear that Aldric was following Darrell's lead. Literally, as in mirroring what Darrell was doing to Aldric. Well, trying his best—if Darrell's assumptions were correct. He couldn't expect to take Darrell as deep as Darrell was swallowing him.

Darrell gave an experimental hum around Aldric's cock, enjoying the full-body shiver it produced in Aldric, who then hummed around him. *Okay.* Darrell stuck a finger in his mouth and wet it with a mixture of his saliva and Aldric's pre-cum. Keeping one hand on the base of Aldric's shaft, he stroked down his cleft with the other. Their position on the bed, with their legs bent to allow access, meant there was no need to part Aldric's cheeks.

Aldric had tightened up again, his sphincter muscles taut around his hole, but he relaxed enough when Darrell rubbed him there, and Darrell slipped his finger in easily, making sure to rub his knuckle against Aldric's walls. He might have been considering angles and depth, but then he wasn't thinking at all when Aldric's finger breached him.

The fuck? Darrell was used to toys and occasionally liked a dildo in his ass while he fucked a partner. Hell, Ric, before Mateo, had enjoyed sliding Darrell's thinnest wand in and out as foreplay, seeing how long Darrell could take it before he flipped Ric over and pounded into him. But this, feeling Aldric's warm living flesh inside him, now retreating, now surging back thicker when Aldric added a second finger — *this* was a different story.

He clenched around the penetration as Aldric was doing to him, wondering if he could take a third digit and if he wanted to take something even bigger that wasn't made of silicone. But he was a top, not a bottom or vers. Taking a dick up the ass wasn't what he did. Wasn't who he was. In his mind, it connected to the feelings of vulnerability he'd had earlier — not so much the injury he'd sustained, but the way Aldric had reacted to it, caring for Darrell as if he were weak. *No.*

He sucked harder, flickering his tongue, wanting Aldric to come first. Repositioning Aldric's top leg and his own hand, he fondled Aldric's balls, then worked his hand over them to tease his taint, wanting to stroke over his prostate from the outside. In some guys it was easy to find. Some liked it and some didn't feel anything. Aldric gave an immediate shudder, and he jerked upward with a sharp, high cry.

The stream of cum that flooded Darrell's mouth seconds later caught him by surprise and almost choked him. He swallowed and carried on sucking until Aldric was writhing under his hands, shaking and babbling out nonsense words. The way he said Darrell's name, the reverence in his voice, lit fires everywhere from Darrell's belly button to his thighs and detonated his release, had it tearing through him like lightning streaking the sky.

Aldric gagged, and Darrell tried to pull free. He should have known that, stubborn as he was, Aldric wouldn't let him set the pace. Aldric clamped his hands to Darrell's butt, holding him where Aldric wanted him, and sucked until he'd milked the last drop from his cock. When Darrell was allowed to slip out, he turned on the bed to check on Aldric and saw the sexiest, most perfect sight ever—Aldric, sweat-mussed hair, flushed face, dazed eyes and swollen lips, from which a trickle of Darrell's cum was escaping.

Aldric raised an unsteady hand to his mouth and wiped at the liquid with the back of it. If he'd intended that as an innocent *what's this happening to little ol' me* gesture, the sly flicker of his eyes toward Darrell's undercut it, and the contradiction, the paradox that was Aldric engulfed Darrell and made him want more.

He scooted up the bed to wrap an arm around Aldric's neck and bring him in for a kiss, knowing he still tasted of Aldric's release, just as Aldric did his. Aldric returned the caress, nuzzling into Darrell. Darrell had been intending to grab a washcloth from the bathroom and clean them up, but Aldric's weight on him bore him down. He barely had time to settle on his back, Aldric on his chest, before Aldric was asleep. It wasn't the most comfortable position for Darrell, with his bruised ribs, but he wouldn't move.

Darrell was tired too—exhausted, even, but his mind kept poking him back to wakefulness every time he dropped off. The case, the second attempt on Aldric, the identity of the thugs—none of that was going through his mind. Instead, how he'd felt when Aldric had played with his ass obsessed him and the thought of Aldric fucking him consumed him. Aldric had barely penetrated him, but Darrell ached to feel him deep inside. Although…he feared he already did, and deeper than any other penetration could ever be.

* * * *

"Darrell?"

Aldric's half-whisper had Darrell wide awake. "What time is it?" he demanded.

"Early. Well, ish. I can take you to your apartment. I have to take the van back." Aldric held out a cup. "Only decaffeinated. I try not to have caffeine in the house."

"You make it sound like a loaded gun." Darrell scanned the nightstand for his. He felt exposed, caught out. Had Aldric watched him sleep? His phone buzzed and a glance at it showed him Mateo's face. He had to change those settings.

"Not answering?"

"It's what voice mail's for." Darrell swung his legs to the floor. Aldric stood there, and Darrell sighed. He needed coffee for this, but... "I was hooking up with him until recently. I broke it off the same day I met you, actually."

"Oh. How did he take it?" Aldric's soft face was creased in concern.

"He never replied to the text. He's been calling."

"*Jesus!*" Aldric cried.

"I've ignored every call. You can see if you like." Darrell gestured at his phone.

"I'm not concerned about that! I'm mad at you treating someone like that." Aldric glared. "Look, there's no time for this now. I've already showered, so go ahead."

The journey to Darrell's residence was silent, Darrell not initiating conversation because he wanted Aldric to focus on the road, and Aldric seemingly agreeing.

"Is that how you end all your relationships?" Aldric asked the second he pulled up at the gate Darrell directed him to and cut the engine.

"I don't have—" He stopped himself saying *relationships*, although it was true. "Look, is all this because you saw me try to talk to him the other day? It wasn't him I was interested in as much as the guy he was with. Wait. That sounds bad. I mean interested professionally. That was Nick Buckman, Buck's son from his first marriage. There was bad blood between father and son, and Buck kicked him out, so my thinking is Nick's back in town to see what he can get now his father's dead." He wished he'd been in a position to answer Mateo's calls, but… "I didn't say anything at the time because I didn't want to worry you. He's not exactly a choir boy."

Aldric's expression was a precursor to his angry words. "How many more times do I have to tell you not to treat me like an idiot, or a snowflake?" he demanded.

"I'm not explaining well." Darrell rubbed his forehead. "Let me get out. I need fresh air and coffee."

A calculating look crossed Aldric's face when they were both outside the vehicle and Darrell glanced along the sidewalk and inside the gate to his complex. "We're right near the coffee stop you use, near your apartment and your parking spot, right? So let's go in and get one. We've got time."

Darrell fell silent. There was so much he wasn't ready for. Everything happening between him and Aldric was moving at lightning speed. Before he could form an answer, Aldric had opened his car door again. "Where are you going?" Darrell demanded.

"What's the point in staying around when you don't listen to me?" Aldric asked. "I've told you more than once I'm not some naïve little flower you have to protect from life. I am capable of standing on my own two feet."

"Is this about the case? It's *dangerous*, Aldric!" Darrell tried to hold back his exasperation. He wanted Aldric to be kept safe, for fuck's sake!

"And remember when I told you that I'm not some behind-closed-doors fuck-buddy? Well, I meant it." Aldric glared at him. "You had a chance and blew it, so that's that."

Darrell's phone rang, and Aldric tilted his chin at it. "I'm not like him—I won't be calling you."

"What?" Darrell didn't believe it. "That's *it*? I *told* you, Aldric! I explained about my family, my job—"

"My family's crap too, but I don't use them as an excuse for being a coward, afraid to try, scared of getting hurt when I want a relationship. I'm living my own life, the best I can."

And with that, Aldric was gone, leaving Darrell staring after him as he drove away.

Chapter Seventeen

For the first time, the jingle of bells on the door handle of the antiques shop as he opened it for the start of a new day didn't fire Aldric with excitement and energy. His mind buzzed like a hive of bees, his emotions swarming in a mass, and he took deep breaths, hoping to calm down. All that did was cause him to inhale the lemongrass and lavender scents that always hung around the place.

Elliot had explained that those herbs and flowers had once been used to keep stored items fresh, and that now makers of air freshener used them in their products, providing a connection to the past. Aldric had thought it charming, but today he found the store musty — stifling, even, when he needed to think clearly. Anger had him clenching his hands into fists, crumpling the paper bag he'd put the puzzle box into that morning. *The dumb decoy box.*

The events of yesterday raced through his head. He hadn't processed them at the time and realized now he hadn't dealt with the assault on him in the alley either.

He should hate this store. He'd felt so full of hope, and even tiny sparks of happiness, when he'd gotten the job here, yet it had resulted in danger and threats and even attacks on him. Maybe there was a curse, but if there was, he doubted it was on the store or even the items from the estate sale. *It's on me.*

"Wish I'd never walked in here that morning," he muttered to the china cabinet, which was filled with plates, dolls and even thimbles of the same material, the grouping a result of the way Elliot liked to arrange the wares by theme or families. "Then I'd —" *Never have met Darrell.*

Aldric had been trying not to think about him but, *bam,* he'd popped up again, and not just because Aldric's body was still purring, wanting to curl up like a cat before a fireplace and bask in the memory of the incredible sex they'd had last night. He didn't know how sex could leave him both sated and sparking with energy, but it had.

Why didn't Darrell see they'd be good together? Well, he couldn't even see that Aldric was capable and independent, not some weakling in need of protection. Darrell seemed to despise that. He thought Aldric had messed up the sting operation. *Did I?* Aldric didn't know. What he did know — well, okay, *felt* — was that if he were more Darrell's type, or what he was seeking in a partner, Darrell would have found it easier to try to be in a real relationship with him. Would have been able to treat him differently from the string of guys he picked up in bars or at the gym or wherever to slake his lust, then play some sort of cat-and-mouse game with, like that Mateo guy.

You're not being fair. Or even rational, his brain told him. "Help me out, then," Aldric ordered it. He gave it time and space while he went about his usual first-on-the-premises routine of making sure that the tea kettle and water jug out on the table in the store were filled and that the miniscule break-room-slash-kitchen that Elliot called a pantry was clean and tidy. He couldn't be angry about having been hired at the store. That was an overreaction. The job had given him many things, like friends and confidence, health insurance and a good, steady income. He needed to work through his anger and fit it into the right place—or purge it altogether.

By the time he'd finished, crumpling up yesterday's newspaper left on the counter into the recycling, squashing it down on top of the box from Elliot's dinner last night, all he'd been able to come up with was that if he could demonstrate he wasn't naïve and in need of help and protection, Darrell would see him differently. And that would work two-fold—if Darrell saw that Aldric had changed and grown, maybe it would show Darrell that *he* could, too. Aldric wandered back into the shop, a vision of a possible future with Darrell, him and Darrell as a couple, tantalizing him. It hung like a ripe fruit, but one on a branch too high to reach easily. "So what do you do when fruit's too high up the tree to pick?"

"Use a ladder?"

Aldric jumped and knocked the paper bag containing the puzzle box from the counter where he'd left it. Elliot just managed to catch it before it hit the floor. "I didn't hear you come in," he gasped, clutching his chest.

"That was evident." Elliot set the bag down and regarded Aldric. "Oh, I can be very stealthy when I need to be. I saw you deep in thought and didn't wish to interrupt." He gave a faint smile. "Genius at work?"

Aldric made a scoffing noise. "I wish. But what did you say — use a ladder? What if there isn't one?" Because he couldn't see one.

"Then I'd suggest making one." Elliot straightened up the small section of leaflets and flyers for other local businesses that he kept in a corner of the counter. "You're being very elliptic today, Aldric. Did anything else happen yesterday while I was out?"

"Oh, how did your meeting go? I forgot to ask," Aldric exclaimed, hoping to get Elliot off the topic.

"It went well. It has the potential to be a profitable and rewarding contact. The gentleman is an interior decorator, always needing to 'source', as he put it, pieces for clients, both commercial and private. He's currently working on a loft conversion apartment Downtown and looking out for Depression glassware, the mass-produced semi-transparent pale-green glass items of the nineteen-thirties. I'm just about to see what pieces I have in stock or in storage or if I have news of any coming up at auctions or sales."

Elliot seemed to have the counter cleaned and arranged to his satisfaction and now turned back to Aldric to continue. "I'm aware you're changing the subject, Aldric, and I would never wish to intrude, of course."

"Of course," Aldric echoed, wondering, not for the first time, about Elliot's courtly, old-fashioned manners and way of speaking. It felt even more like something out of an old black-and-white movie than usual today.

"But if you explain, maybe I can help? I can see you're perturbed and I would like to help ease that."

"I… Yes." Relief rushed into Aldric like the tide into a rockpool. "Something did happen yesterday, well, has been happening, and I think I do need help."

"I see." Elliot's demeanor sharpened, his tawny-brown eyes brightening behind their wire-framed glasses. "I wonder if this is a case of three heads being better than two? If so, Jonas should be along any minute now…"

The bells at the door tinkled right on cue as the third Intrinsic Value employee entered and stopped in his tracks. He probably wasn't expecting to see his boss and co-worker waiting for him, about to pounce. He looked from one to another.

"No, nothing's wrong," Elliot assured him. "At least, I think not. Aldric is about to explain something and where he needs help on it."

"I'm in." Jonas' reply came instantly.

Elliot clapped Jonas on the shoulder as he walked past him to lock the door and flip the sign to closed. "But first, please tell us how the interview went at the university. Or is it a college? I can never keep up with these changes in academia." Elliot made himself seem older than he was.

"Oh yes!" Aldric exclaimed. He felt ashamed for being so wrapped up in his own stuff that he hadn't asked how things had gone for Jonas.

"Oh, I think it went well." Jonas' modest half-smile came and went. "I feel good about my chances."

"They'd be lucky to have you on their faculty, and you deserve much more than filling in as a replacement for someone halfway through the semester," Elliot told him warmly.

"Well, we can't always get what we want, no matter how much we want it or how much we have to bring to it." Jonas suddenly sounded bleak. "But we can try."

He was a natural teacher, patient and clear, and Aldric had wondered why he wasn't working in the field his qualifications were in. His theory was that Jonas had been burned out, had needed a break from teens or young adults and was trying to make a living from his side-line. "You miss it," he deduced. "Is the university at the Hill where you just interviewed like the sort of place you worked at before?"

"Aldric!" Elliot scolded. "Quit stalling!"

Elliot had the occasional lapse from his old-fashioned ways and into more modern speech, Aldric had noticed. He nodded and launched into the story, trying hard to leave nothing out. Elliot exclaimed when Aldric described how the two men had tried to snatch him.

"Attempted abduction? In broad daylight?" he gasped. "Sorry, I interrupted, Aldric. Go on."

Some details Aldric had to blur, of course, but he felt both men understood what was between him and Darrell. *What had been*, he corrected himself. He also felt neither man would judge him or recoil from him.

"Hmm." Jonas took off his tortoise-shell-framed glasses and rubbed them with a tissue. "Whatever's happening, and something is, it's connected to the Buckman estate purchases, correct?" Aldric nodded, and Jonas continued, "Let's narrow it down. It isn't all the contents of Buck Buckman's study that Elliot bought. As amusing as they are, the finger traps he used on guests and the 'priceless sculpture' he showed off to them that collapsed when they were near it, causing consternation and shock, aren't part of it."

He chuckled. "Though I must say, I would have liked to see the 'first folio Shakespeare' whose pages fluttered out and crumbled when the cover was opened! I wonder how often he used that trick on the unwary, and how they reacted! But our concern is only the puzzle boxes, that are in and of themselves, cheap toys with no precious value." He pointed at the one on the counter. "Like that one, for instance. Common wood and a common item. We can narrow our focus to a finer point yet — to the one box said to be his favorite."

"So let's get to work." Elliot undid his cuffs and rolled up his sleeves. "Luckily I still have all the items here and didn't take them to the safety deposit."

Fetched from the safe and spread out along the countertop of an antiques store, the wooden boxes looked cheaper and flimsier than ever.

"This hexagonal one?" Elliot checked. Aldric nodded. "Jonas, take note."

"Thank you both for this," Aldric said, appreciating the support more than he could explain. "You have no reason to help, and any other boss I've ever had would have fired me for bringing all this trouble to his door."

Elliot shook his head. "None of this is your fault, Aldric, any more than it is mine for purchasing the items in the first place. If anything, more blame attaches to me for not getting rid of them. But even though neither of us started this, we'll end it, yes?"

"All for one and one for all?" Jonas added, perplexing Aldric. "The Three Musketeers, Aldric."

The reference to a chocolate bar confused Aldric even more, but he fetched stools, and he, Elliot and Jonas took four boxes each. Elliot took a gilt sandglass from a shelf and turned it over.

"We'll work on a box until the sand runs out, then switch," he declared.

Aldric cheated a little by starting with the rectangular one he'd opened before. It had taken him a while when he'd played around with it last week, but now it was simple to slide the lid back — and not be frustrated when it didn't move all the way — then forward as far as it would go, then back to the closed position. The next move was to the left, and, when he moved the lid to the right after that, it glided completely off. The box was empty.

"Uggh!" Elliot drummed his fingers in frustration on the counter either side of the box he was working on. "I heard a click, but then I did something and heard another click, and nothing's moving!"

"That's the difficulty, locking it again without knowing how you half-opened it," Aldric replied.

They managed to open two more as the morning went on, but neither of them was the box in question. That was easily the most ornate and Elliot studied it from several angles and different distances, much the same as Aldric had the works of art in the museum.

"I think it must have something to do with the inlay squares," Elliot said at last. "They're applique, not just different marquetry wood mosaic."

He began pushing at the middle strips, perhaps hoping to push them out as he had the square box he'd solved, but nothing happened. Jonas tried twisting the top one way while twisting the box another, in the same manner in which *he'd* opened a round box and found a netsuke miniature sculpture inside, but that did nothing in this case.

"This is infuriating, and I don't see us getting anywhere," Elliot said at last.

"My cousin Selena would just smash it," Aldric admitted.

"No." Jonas put out a hand, as if Aldric were about to do just that. "Oh, not because of any curse, but from what I've been reading, some bigger ones like this were used to carry secret documents or messages and had thief traps in case anyone tried to smash them open."

"Like what?"

"Dye that destroyed the paper inside," Jonas told Elliot. "I'm convinced this box contains something."

"Thief trap..." Aldric closed his eyes to think. "That's what we need. To draw anyone who wants the box to it, but under our terms, not theirs." He opened his eyes again. "What if we displayed the boxes somewhere, but just for a short space of time? Luring whoever's after them to attempt to steal them, or this one, and we catch him red-handed?"

Catch Nick Buckman. Aldric had been thinking over what Darrell had said about the guy, whose own father had kicked him out, being back in town to see what he could get his hands on now his father was gone. Darrell's face, when he'd hinted that Nick wasn't exactly a model citizen... He thought the man was behind it—Aldric was convinced. Aldric did too.

"It seems a good idea, but shouldn't we involve the police?" Jonas asked.

"We tried that and got nowhere." Aldric swallowed. That sentence was a good description of what had happened between him and Darrell. "So let's try again, and this time do better."

"If you're absolutely sure," Elliot said slowly.

Aldric wasn't, but he nodded anyway. "Let's do this."

Chapter Eighteen

"You're great for business!" Enzo, the owner of the Spectrum Art Space, told Elliot, clapping him on the back later that afternoon and beaming at all the visitors wandering around the artifacts that Aldric, Jonas and Elliot had laid out.

"Oh, I think business is good here as a rule. This static display of old trinkets is nothing in the grand scheme of things, which is why I very much appreciate you ceding us this hall," Elliot replied to his friend.

Aldric had supposed a gallery or art space owner would be older, and more of a businessman, like Elliot, especially with him being a buddy and the only reason they'd been given a venue for their pop-up exhibition. Or that he'd be wearing a suit and have a quiet, soft manner, like the curators Aldric had seen at the museum. Instead, the man had the ponytail, goatee and small rectangular glasses of a hipster, and the enthusiasm and energy of a middle-schooler.

The space, part of the first floor of the Navarro Building downtown, was just as fashionable, with its different rooms showing a variety of exhibitions and displays, from immersive and experiential art to interactive installations, mostly by local artists and collectives. "The whole Spectrum," as Enzo put it, making the reason for the choice of name clear.

Aldric barely knew what the words meant or even if these fields of art were very different, and despite having taken quick peeps into the other rooms, with their neon lights and experimental music, was still not much the wiser. He could have spent longer in each space and had Enzo or even the artists themselves show him around. The multi-location virtual walk through an alternative San Antonio looked very interesting, if puzzling, but Aldric wouldn't leave the Intrinsic Value artifacts display for long. He kept his eyes glued to the table in the middle of their room, the one holding the hexagonal box.

Elliot touched his arm. "You can take a break, Aldric. We do have others to watch the items."

Aldric still couldn't believe Elliot had hired a security guard to escort them from the store to the gallery when they'd conveyed the artifacts earlier, or that the same guard was here now, standing out like a sore thumb amid the much more colorfully dressed and animated visitors.

"Is this how rock stars feel?" he'd asked, bemused, when he and Jonas had arrived with their boxes. By no means a confident, at-ease person, he'd been more watchful since the attack in the alley and the attempt on him at the mission. The idea that there could be someone lying in wait made him shiver. *This is your idea, remember?* he'd told himself both on arrival and at intervals throughout the afternoon, whenever he'd felt any prickle of suspicion or warning.

"No. Thank you, but I'd rather stay," Aldric replied to his employer. "After all, this was my doing. Well, my idea."

He couldn't claim any credit for putting on the exhibition or drumming up the publicity for it that had attracted the steady trickle of visitors. He just hoped Elliot hadn't had to spend too much money to get ads on the local radio to get the news out. Word of mouth had contributed as well, he supposed. There'd been people calling into Intrinsic Value since midday, curious to ask them about the 'haunted' or 'cursed' objects.

The three of them had come up with the tale that accompanied the announcement of the one-time-only exhibition, and it seemed to have captured people's imaginations. Elliot had been strict about them not using any untruths that they didn't have to in their advertising of the event, and they'd only told one, but the description of the incidents surrounding the artifacts was gripping. Aldric felt sorry that Randa Buckman had been dragged into it—not just mentioned by name, as the widow of the deceased owner, but that a couple of reporters had tried to reach her too, to add to the story.

"So it's kinda like when they opened Tutankhamun's tomb?" a woman was asking now, pointing at the boxes. "Only in this case, not disturbing the possessions but separating the owner from them unleashed the curse?"

"It's one theory," Elliot agreed, his more formal, correct tone making the woman's enthusiasm sound more breathless.

"And does the buyer they're going to know about it?" asked her friend. "Or is that why he wants them? He collects macabre stuff?"

"What makes you think it's a he?" Aldric put in. This was the one thing they'd invented, that the goods were being shipped out of state first thing tomorrow, to a collector of curios who'd bought the whole lot. Aldric, thinking of Buck's widow and how she'd cried on the phone the other day, had left a message at the Buckman estate telling her about the exhibition in case she hadn't caught the announcements. She hadn't been available to him or to give any comments to any reporters or journalists, so she might have been away. Her assistant had promised to pass his message on, however, and this way, she'd have another chance to see the items.

"It's good to see you interacting with people like that." Elliot smiled at Aldric. "When you first started at Intrinsic Value, you were rather diffident at dealing with customers, remember? I recall you blushing and stammering when you tried to reply to questions about an item or its price, or even asking the customer to wait until I or Jonas were free to attend to them."

"And look at you now," Jonas agreed. "You even gave a mini-interview to those high school kids wanting to include this in their assignment!"

"Well, someone had to," Aldric joked. Elliot didn't like the limelight. When they'd been planning earlier, Jonas had suggested Elliot feature in the short video announcement about the Buckman acquisitions exhibition that they were putting on the store's website and sending to customers via email, among other things, but he'd refused. He didn't like having his photograph taken. Aldric didn't know why, when Elliot was so distinguished-looking.

He thought about what Elliot and Jonas had just said. It was true that Aldric felt more at ease than he used to, more comfortable not just in his skin, but about taking up space in the world. He was a determined person who could fight, despite the occasional stutter on his lips, the thudding of his heart or the shakiness in his limbs, when it came to something he really wanted.

Something like Darrell. He'd put his foot down there and stood up for himself, because he wanted all of Darrell, and not just the bits Darrell gave him behind closed doors. *And if that means I end up with no part of him at all? Well, tough.* The thought was bleak and cold, but he'd have to live with it, and surely the feeling of loss that wanted to open up like a sinkhole at his feet and engulf him would lessen in time. *Right?*

He wished Darrell were there, were with him on this, though. He held in a snort of laughter, imagining Darrell at this place, taking in the different exhibitions. He'd never seen Darrell at the gym but imagined him in that sort of setting, his biceps flexing as he worked with weights, or his lean glutes contracting and lengthening as he did squats. Darrell was proficient with a firearm too. Aldric had read the write-up about the recent Mafia arrests and the police officers' roles in it, rereading the description of how quickly Officer Williams had drawn his weapon. It gave Aldric more fodder for his fantasies, picturing Darrell at the gun range. He tried hard not to think that fantasies were all he'd be left with, if Darrell remained closeted and never came out.

Oh. Thinking about Darrell and the police had given him an idea. "Elliot." He spoke quietly to avoid being overheard. "Instead of me having a break, what if we gave the security guard one?"

"He's due for one," Elliot agreed. "Ah. I think I see what you're getting at. That while the cat's away, the mice...how shall I put it...might *pounce.*"

It wasn't that amusing, and the situation was far from a joke, but Elliot's silly words brought a smile to Aldric's face and he nodded. The tall, square-shouldered guard no longer being in the room changed the atmosphere, making Aldric edgy. Now, everyone approaching the collection of knickknacks, from cynical teenagers to curious adults, was a potential threat, and within five minutes, Aldric's tense shoulders were aching.

But nothing happened.

Elliot looked paler and more drawn as the evening went on, and Aldric felt guilty and foolish. He caught the yawn Elliot tried to conceal and saw Jonas sneak more than one look at his watch. The foot traffic died off in their exhibition hall and the art space as a whole, the place becoming quieter.

"Guys." Enzo stood there. "We're not far from closing time."

And we have nothing to show for it. "I'm really sorry," Aldric started, and Elliot shook his head.

"It was a good idea. Just because nothing came of it doesn't negate that. At the very least, we had some publicity for the store. I anticipate a good number of walk-ins as a result of this. Curiosity is a great motivator."

"Thank you. Look, I'm happy to pack away if you two want to go?" Aldric offered. It was the least he could do.

"If you're sure?" Elliot beckoned the guard over. "I feel relatively easy about it, as you'll have Mr. Smith here standing watch." He checked that the man knew his instructions for removal and transport of the items.

"Well, see you tomorrow," Jonas said, as he too took his leave. "Sorry it didn't work out, Aldric."

It didn't take long to clear away the curios. It wasn't as though each had to be carefully packaged in bubble wrap and nestled into its own box that was then filled with packing peanuts. Mr. Smith, if that was his real name, helped, and even let Aldric sit up front with him in the van he was driving to transport the goods to Elliot's safe deposit place.

Downtown was lively and loud, and Aldric realized they were just north of it, in the 'gayborhood', when he saw two guys walking along holding hands, one pointing toward a bar and his slighter taller boyfriend shaking his head and indicating another, across the street. Aldric wondered who won and thought they probably both had. This was Darrell's neighborhood. He must go to the bars and clubs around here, hooking up—and discarding. Aldric turned away from the window. He didn't go to this area much and now he'd make sure he came even less.

They drove through the city in silence until they were out of the downtown area.

"These antiques. Artifacts. Goods. I'd have thought they'd be in a bank vault, or somewhere…not here," the guard said as they arrived off San Antonio's north side, before the Hill Country. He spared a glance for his passenger. "You do know it's kind of isolated out here, right?"

Even if he hadn't, he could have worked it out, but Aldric just shrugged. "As long as the place is secure." He hoped it was, because, for him, the evening wasn't over. *"Nothing came of it." "It didn't work out."* Elliot's and Jonas' words replayed in his head, and Aldric added *'Yet,'* to them, because he still had plans.

Shrugging, the guard pulled into the dirt lot in front of the building. Aldric hadn't known what to expect of a safety deposit facility, his imagination veering from a state-of-the-art fortress with crisscrossing laser beams to a row of self-storage units in a yard behind a metal gate. This was big and looked like a warehouse. There were only a couple of other vehicles in the shadowy lot, at the back where employees would park.

"Thanks," Aldric said when Mr. Smith took most of the artifacts from the van. He juggled his armful of stuff with the main door keycard and pad to enter the code. He'd memorized it along with the one he'd need for the Intrinsic Value room, when he found it. Mr. Smith scanned the barely lit foyer inside.

"Should be a guard," he commented, pointing a foot at the desk and chair.

"He must be on his rounds?"

The twist to his companion's lips suggested the guard was making use of a more comfortable chair somewhere. Aldric had worked night shifts along with day shifts and had used the former to catch up on sleep, for all he should have been busy. Someone to show them to the depository would have been useful, and someone to turn on the lights even more so.

Elliot's storage room, when they found it, was bigger than Aldric had expected. It had two or three shelves on each of its three walls, running most of their length, and high steel shelving units were fitted across the room in tiers, leaving narrow aisles between each one. They reminded Aldric of library stacks. He'd been in nearly empty libraries, when sounds were amplified and echoed, but none had been this cold or this creepy, making him shiver on entry.

"Thanks. I have to unpack these and, erm, catalog them," he told Mr. Smith, hoping the guy wouldn't ask how or why, or worse, what were the mysterious-looking shrouded objects on the higher stacks. "Mr. Douglas doesn't expect you to wait. Thanks again." He nodded when the man asked him if he had his own transport. *Saying nothing isn't telling a lie.*

It got colder and darker and much more frightening once he was alone, the door closed via the keypad, sealing him in the windowless space. Every squeak and scurry had him tense and every rustle and thump made him retreat behind another row. This was stupid, just like his other idea had been stupid. He glared at Buck Buckman's former possessions where he'd arranged them on a side shelf, spread out in a long row from the middle to stretch to the back of the room. He'd become obsessed with these puzzle boxes ever since he'd been attacked. A natural reaction, maybe, but stupid. No one was coming.

Or so he told himself until he couldn't anymore, because the metallic noise had been the main door opening, the short thumps had been footsteps and the rattling at the depository door was someone trying to open it. Aldric grabbed a lamp base to use as a weapon and stood to the side. When the metal door rattled in its frame, the result of whoever was outside trying to force it open, Aldric, his heart thumping like a kettledrum, hit the command on the keypad to open the door. Hoping for the element of surprise, he raised his weapon, prepared to hit whoever was breaking in over the head, only for his hands to freeze near his shoulder.

"*Darrell?*"

Chapter Nineteen

Aldric! He'd been right. Darrell lowered his gun but didn't holster it. He pushed himself inside the lock-room, taking Aldric with him. "How does this door lock?" he snapped, relief making him brittle. He'd been thinking about Aldric, and him and Aldric, and him without Aldric, almost constantly. And yet now that he was here, in front of Darrell, Darrell was still groping his way through the mental fog of the last twelve hours. "Well?"

Wordlessly, Aldric reached for a button on the keypad and the door jerked sideways from the frame, closing the entrance to the room.

"Before you ask me how I'm here, I heard it on the news. There was no one at the gallery place mentioned and the store was deserted, and when they said the goods would be kept at a safety deposit for one night, I remembered Elliot mentioning the place. So I knew you'd be here." Darrell hated that he was still speaking in short, jerky sentences and that what they were here for had nothing to do with his feelings, with the things he knew he had to talk about. *Or perhaps it does, in some ways.*

Working out what Aldric had planned had put years on Darrell. He had no idea how Aldric and the rest of the Intrinsic Value people had been able to organize this so quickly, but they had. "'Are you brave enough to brave a curse?'" he quoted, mimicking the inane blonde newsreader.

"How did you get in?" Aldric asked.

"The guard's mooching around the parking lot and all it took was a flash of my badge. He told me which unit." Darrell slid his gun into the holster at the small of his back and wiped his hand across his mouth. He hadn't realized how scared he'd been until he'd caught sight of Aldric's tangle of soft brown hair and big brown eyes on the other side of the door. Had it really only been this morning that Aldric had left him standing by the side of the road, having delivered his ultimatum? It felt a lot longer. "Why?" he asked.

"Why this? I thought it would work. Flush Nick Buckman out." Aldric waved a hand at the room. "It was stupid. Is that why you're here?"

"Nick B — ?" Yeah, that wasn't the important part of what Aldric had said. "Not because I think you're stupid, no. You're not. You're very intelligent."

"Like, I'm the sensitive, artistic one?"

Darrell shook his head in incomprehension. "I couldn't let you be in danger. And not because I think you're weak and that I'm strong." He struggled for words, to put into speech all the things he'd been brooding on since Aldric had left him, his words hurting like blows. "Jesus, Aldric! I didn't want to be doing this. I need more time."

"To string me along? Tell me that you're working on things, that I have to be patient, to understand, to wait?"

That would be the weak way to deal with it. "More time to get my shit together. To find the words to tell you that although we haven't known each other long, I care about you. Very much, and…and I find you fascinating. And frustrating. And a whole bunch of other things that I have to say to you. But now, now that I'm with you, and you're here with those big brown eyes and that stubborn jut of your chin…"

Aldric rubbed his chin, as if testing it. "Now, what?"

"All the thoughts left in my head about you are revolving around this." Darrell reached out a hand to Aldric's and slotted his fingers through Aldric's, then held it, loosely, as if testing their fit. It was good. He squeezed, and Aldric squeezed back, the contact warming Darrell through. Darrell uncurled his fingers and steepled them, Aldric copying him, fitting his palm against Darrell's, never breaking their bond.

"Your thoughts are about holding hands with me?" Aldric blinked. "Like—"

"Like what?"

"Nothing. Just something I saw. Out in the street, in the open."

Aldric was the one who blushed, yet Darrell's face heated. Even if Aldric hadn't meant it as a rebuke, it stung. "Can we sit down?" he asked.

"I don't think there are any seats." Aldric turned to go look, and because Darrell was still holding his hand, he was pulled along with him.

Darrell couldn't see any chairs and doubted there would be any. Impatient, he sank to sit against a metal row, this time bringing Aldric down with him. The floor was hard and cold to sit on and the room dim, the only light coming from somewhere overhead and out in the narrow corridor. "There's a lot I have to say. Well, when I've worked it out. But I least I realize there's a lot I have to work out, right?"

"Yes?" Aldric sounded as confused as Darrell felt. "Are you going to kiss me?"

"Do you want me to?" Darrell moved close enough to touch the tip of his nose to Aldric's, and the bump of Aldric's nose slid from his when Aldric nodded. Relieved by the knowledge that Aldric was giving him another chance, Darrell closed the gap between them, which was easy enough to do when he was already so close that he could feel Aldric's breath on his face. The touch of his lips to Aldric's was tender, asking, not demanding, and almost hesitant in a way that Darrell never let himself be.

The caress started out reminding Darrell of their last night together when they'd sixty-nined and he'd led and Aldric had followed. *Had copied, even.* But now Aldric took the lead, sweeping his tongue into Darrell's mouth, searching the recesses. He also broke the kiss, in his own time, leaving Darrell alone.

"That was good."

Darrell was glad the light was enough to see Aldric's smile.

"But it's going to take more than that. It's going to—" Aldric broke off and clutched Darrell. "Did you hear that? Please tell me I imagined it."

"I wish I could, babe." Darrell pulled Aldric in tight to whisper in his ear, "But I can't, because you didn't." The noise came again—from the small entrance lobby just inside the main door, Darrell estimated. He'd been half-expecting it, anyway. "Someone's breaking in." He stood, trying to work out what the thuds and bangs could be. The light outside in the corridor went off with a *ting* and small gleams of emergency lights came on. He'd seen the strips along the floor and high on the walls, and now saw the actual glow of them in here. He stumbled a little as Aldric, now on his feet too, clutched him.

"I thought this plan was stupid because it didn't work," Aldric whispered, "but now I *know* it's stupid because it did work."

"Here." Darrell twisted and slid his backup gun free of his shoulder holster. "Take this. No, take it," he urged when Aldric shook his head. "I've got mine." He pulled that out too.

"It's not that. I can't use one."

"You can't—?" Darrell shook his head. "Hold the gun like this." He curled Aldric's fingers around the Glock. "You've seen one used, right?"

"They were firing them a lot in the movie we saw the other night. Well, what we saw of it…" Aldric rasped, his hands shaking as he held the weapon.

As dire as things were, Darrell had to smile at that. "Good choice then, huh? And I nearly chose mini-golf for our date. If you have to, just point and shoot. The Glock'll do the rest."

"Darrell." Aldric licked his lips, and Darrell wanted to chase Aldric's tongue with his own. "I'm glad you're here with me."

"I am, too." The thought of Aldric going through this alone, even though he'd set it in motion, was frightening. "I wish this wasn't happening," he muttered. He wished instead that he had time and the tools to sort through all the stuff he'd told Aldric he needed to. There was a lot of it, and it was all twisted together, his upbringing and family beliefs casting a long shadow over everything, from his choice of career to the way he lived his life. *Compartmentalized. Not living it fully.*

Digging down into the past was complicated, re-evaluating the present was tough and reshaping a possible future was terrifying. Fear of the unknown was strong. At least he knew his family and his place in it. Would speaking honestly and openly to them about the kind of life he wanted mean cutting ties with them? And what about his job?

Noises at the door brought his focus to the here and now, and the clear and present danger coming at him and Aldric. "Where's the Buckman stuff?" he mouthed to Aldric, who pointed to the long shelf running the length of the right wall. Darrell signaled to Aldric to move to the other side of the room and crouch behind a stack. If Aldric had asked why that one, he'd have explained that it was far enough from the door that whoever was coming in wouldn't see them unless they searched the room, and close enough to the door for them to duck from row to row and make escape relatively easy.

He checked that he could see through gaps in the items and through spaces in the stacks themselves. A box had been placed against the wall not far from the end of their row, so Darrell grabbed at it to heave it in front of them for extra cover, finding it heavier than he'd expected. He wondered what it contained.

"They don't have a key card, do they? And they don't know the code. How will they get in?" Aldric breathed.

"They cut the power." Darrell made sure his flashlight was ready. "Any backup that came on will be weaker, so the locks are easier to disable. Or they could have paid off the guard for entrance."

Or wrench off the locks, he amended a second later, interpreting the noises just outside. The place must have safeguards, such as alarms that went off when any break-in was attempted, so anyone wanting in would have to work quickly—getting in, getting what they came for and getting away before any response came. Darrell wasn't pinning his hopes on the night guard he'd seen out front.

The door slid open with a metallic screech and stopped partway. Two black-clad figures took over from the reluctant mechanism and forced it most of the way to the side, then entered. For all the crap about the curse, or haunting, or ghosts, they were definitely human and, Darrell thought, familiar. Aldric's poke to his side confirmed that he recognized them too—and caught Darrell on a bruise the slightly shorter person had inflicted on his ribs. He gave a nod to show he understood. Were the crooks going to make this look supernatural too? Spray more pentagrams around? Smash things up?

The men paused, looking around. Darrell thought he knew why. They didn't know where the stuff they were after was. Did they even know what it looked like? Maybe not, and the room's shelves and units held a good amount of stuff. The taller of the two thieves said something, but not to his companion. He turned and spoke out into the corridor. *Crap! How many more are in this gang?* Darrell tightened his hold on his Smith & Wesson.

A third person entered the depository after the first two and stood between them, shining a flashlight along the shelves until the beam hit the items the crooks wanted. "Over there," she directed.

She. Randa Buckman. Shit. Things fell into place like a ton of bricks. He'd felt her grieving widow act was just that and hadn't believed in the 'my dead husband is haunting and cursing things' schtick. No wonder there'd been no damage to the main house, only the pool house—Randa valued the former too much to vandalize it.

Had she attempted to get the artifacts back from Intrinsic Value, that first evening, and smashed up what Aldric had been carrying in her rage before hiring these thugs? If so, she'd been the one to assault Aldric.

If Darrell was surprised, Aldric appeared to be more so. Startled, he pointed toward the figures standing a few feet away—pointed with the hand that held the gun and knocked the end of the barrel into the box Darrell had dragged in front of them. It wasn't loud, as noises went, and not as loud as Randa's thugs had been when forcing the door, but it was audible.

Aldric jolted backward, as if trying to get out of the way of the box, and stumbled. Before Darrell could grab him and steady him, he dropped his gun onto the floor with a clatter that echoed. Worse, in attempting to snatch it back up again, Aldric kicked it.

"Step forward. Slowly," one of the thugs shouted, and Aldric, decent, law-abiding Aldric, obeyed, standing and stepping out from their cover then moving forward.

"No!" Darrell cried, seeing the man draw and aim. He dived in front of Aldric and the bullet that had been meant for Aldric hit Darrell in the chest instead, sending him spinning and crashing to the floor.

"Darrell!" screamed Aldric.

Neither Aldric's cry nor the bullet to his chest stopped Darrell firing and hitting the guy with the gun. Darrell got him in the shoulder, making him drop his weapon and scream in pain. It also took him out of the game, much like Darrell, who lay gasping on his front, one hand pressed to his torso, feeling for damage.

"Guy back there, kick his gun over here. Slowly," ordered the second man.

Aldric obeyed once more, inching toward Darrell, his face agonized, lurching and tripping as he pushed Darrell's gun away with one foot. Glaring at Randa, who laughed at Aldric's clumsiness, Darrell almost missed what Aldric was doing. He was kicking Darrell's gun away, as ordered, sure, but also placing the gun Darrell had given him under Darrell's outstretched arm, carefully and unobtrusively. Darrell hadn't even seen him pick it up, but there it was, a small lump of deadly metal next to his flesh.

"Kid, we'll let the two of you go if you bring out the box," Randa offered. "You know which one, I'm betting."

Darrell exchanged a look with Aldric. *Do it. They won't let us out alive anyway.*

Aldric raised his hands and edged around the metal stack to the shelves along the wall. He found the hexagonal box and placed it on the floor, where it stood small among much larger objects lying about, and took a few steps to the door. "Darrell, come on," he said, looking over at him, then the trio. "What? You said we could go."

"And you believed that?" sneered the taller goon.

"No," Aldric replied…in the same instant that he snatched up a huge square metal statue from the floor and whacked the guy over the head with it. The thug went down hard. Darrell hoped his head would hurt like hell.

Darrell levelled his weapon at Randa and got to his feet. "Put your hands up, Mrs. Buckman."

Her mouth dropped open, and she sputtered. "They...they made me do it! I'm innocent! I'm so glad—"

"Hands up," Darrell snapped. "And mouth shut. You have the right to remain silent—"

Mrs. Buckman glared but raised her hands. She didn't speak again.

"You use these before?" Darrell brandished zip ties and indicated the injured man.

Aldric shook his head. "Maybe if we'd stayed for the second movie." He started to tremble as Darrell saw to the guy. "You were shot. I saw you fall and—"

"Bulletproof vest," Darrell told him, hoping to comfort him somewhat but not lie. "So it didn't penetrate through, but the site of impact hurts like a motherfucker." Darrell moved over to Mrs. Buckman. "Hands behind your back."

After she had complied, Darrell zip-tied her wrists, then shouted for the guard. "You okay?" he asked when the guy limped into sight.

"Fuckers hit me!" the guard answered, rubbing the back of his head.

"D'you call nine-one-one?" Darrell asked.

"Yeah," came the guard's reply "I'm not stupid."

"That's debatable," Darrell grumbled, then looked at Mrs. Buckman. "Lady, what the fuck is so important about that goddamn puzzle box?"

"A will," Randa spat. "Buck apparently left a will hidden, deeding the house and estate to his fucking son to say sorry for how he treated him. I found little clues hidden in the rest of his crap that let me know what he did."

Aldric's trembling turned into a tooth-jarring full-body shake and he heaved a few times, although he didn't throw up. His glasses flew off with his convulsions, and Darrell caught them and put them on for him.

"Thinking about getting contacts," Aldric mumbled.

"Don't you dare," Darrell warned him. "Love your sexy specs." He hugged Aldric tight and was still holding him close when the cops arrived, with Elliot on their heels. As they stared, Darrell stroked Aldric's neck and head, cradling him to his chest, and stared back.

Chapter Twenty

Aldric had fainted once, a few years earlier, on the high school track after being forced to sprint in the hot sun. He remembered the feeling, like a lid up on high was coming down, enclosing him in a little jar, making the sight of the track and the other kids blurry and the sound of their voices and the coach's yelling echoey, until the top came right down, squashing him to the ground.

He remembered it vividly, because it was happening again, the room growing smaller and narrower, the slam of feet and the bark of orders becoming quieter and the air getting thinner. Before, he hadn't been pressed tight to another man's body like he was now, breathing in Darrell's scent that was both familiar and arousing. It would be nice to let go into that.

No. He fought against it. He was an adult, responsible for the mess he'd made. The police would have questions to ask about the assault he'd committed. He couldn't leave the cleaning up to Darrell. Aldric shifted and felt the cup of Darrell's hand around the back of his neck and the press of his lips on the top of his head. When he turned around, he stared straight into two faces he knew, both of them wide-eyed and open-mouthed.

Sean, Darrell's partner, and Elliot, Aldric's boss.

"Darrell?" Sean lowered his gun. He wasn't in uniform but had his badge around his neck and a police armband on. "Dispatch called me when you called in. What the hell's going on?"

"Whatever is going on, could it not be in here?" Elliot stepped forward. "I believe Aldric would benefit from fresh air."

"He needs to answer questions and undergo medical triage," a uniformed officer replied from the middle of the bustle.

"Both of which he can do perfectly well outside," Elliot snapped.

Things went a little hazy on the short walk through the building, but Aldric did feel better in the fresh air, even with questions being asked of him from all sides, making him swing his head around to answer. Elliot, next to him, backed him up, stressing the plan they'd all concocted. Aldric wondered what Elliot was doing there, but the similarity of this night to the one when he'd been attacked in the alley made him suppose Elliot was notified of any trouble in his safety deposit vault.

A police jacket appeared around his shoulders and a plastic chair was found for him. Darrell didn't get either, Aldric noticed, so he pulled him down onto the seat, as small as it was, and tucked half the jacket over one of his shoulders. That caused a silence. Everyone stopped talking and froze, the scene illuminated by the blue light of the emergency vehicles parked in the lot.

"What was I doing?" Darrell was addressing not just his partner but the group of cops, Aldric felt. "I came to back up Aldric. I realized what *he* was doing and wasn't about to let him go through with this on his own."

Aldric focused on Elliot rather than sweeping his gaze over the police officers, because the range of looks on their faces was narrow and none of them was positive.

"I should have guessed there was another step to your plan," said Elliot. "It seems Darrell knows you better than I do."

"That right?" Sean asked, glancing from the other officers to Darrell. "Darrell?"

"I should hope so." Darrell slotted his fingers through Aldric's, as he'd done inside the depository room. "Considering he's my boyfriend." He nudged his head into Aldric's. "Aren't you?"

For a moment, Aldric couldn't speak. His heart was thumping too loudly and too far, filling his whole body. He had to wait for it to calm down to speak. "Yes."

And that was it. Just one little word, but with such huge implications, and one that they were starting right here, with Darrell's fellow officers as witnesses. "It's not going to be easy," he muttered, understanding something of what Darrell was setting in motion, but only able to guess the impact it would have on all areas of his life. Darrell would know its weight, though. He'd said he needed more time, but life didn't always allow a person what they wanted at their own pace.

Aldric felt humbled. Had Darrell been thinking things over since Aldric had left him, like Aldric had nonstop?

"Oh, I know that." Darrell stood slowly and swept his gaze over the milling police officers and beyond them, as if taking in the city, the place he lived, and where his family did too, but when he swung back to Aldric, the light in his eyes was just for him. "Boy, do I. You're bossy, for one thing. And for another, I think I've got at least one rib broken this time."

"When you saved me?" The memory came back, Darrell jumping in front of the bullet that had been aimed at Aldric. "You took a bullet for me!" he cried.

"Aldric?" Elliot's voice quivered.

"Well, you saved me right back," Darrell replied. "You tricked them and slipped me a gun and took one of those thugs out with a goddam statue, for Christ's sake!"

Aldric raised an eyebrow at Darrell. At his *boyfriend*. "Did you just almost quote *Pretty Woman*? Because the actual word they use is *rescue*. 'She rescues him right back.'"

Darrell started to laugh, only to stop, groan and clutch his side. "Yep, definitely broken," he judged.

This caused a flurry of activity, Darrell taken off to the ambulance, and the EMT insisting on examining him. "You owe me for this, babe," he mouthed at Aldric over their fussing.

"Hey." Sean was standing there before Aldric could reply. "Look, I'll get straight to it. I don't know how to react to this." He waved a finger between his partner and Aldric. "I don't know how anyone at the station will."

"I can guess." Darrell winced as he tried to slip his shirt back on. "SAPD isn't a beacon of tolerance for any kind of minority."

"Then why?" Sean demanded.

"Because I'm more afraid of losing a chance with Aldric than I am of what people might say or do."

"But you only just met him." Sean sat on the edge of the ambulance, looking from Darrell to Aldric. "It's what, love at first sight?"

Darrell laughed, then groaned. "Ow. Ribs. Would it make it better if it was? I don't know, Sean. Do you know, Aldric?"

Aldric thought about it. *Love.* They'd barely just met each other! He considered all the things he knew about Darrell and all the things he liked about him. They were one and the same. And Darrell had felt strongly enough about him to take that frightening, life-changing step forward. But was that love?

"I think that's what grows. What blooms. Maybe. With luck. But first you have to give the seeds a chance," Aldric suggested.

"And all I know is I want a chance. I don't expect everyone to understand or, God knows, approve, but, Sean…" Darrell shrugged. "I have to try."

Was Sean going to say he didn't want to be Darrell's partner any longer? Could cops do that? Aldric had no idea and it wasn't as though he could ask any of the officers on the scene for information. They were starting to show signs of leaving anyway, with their attackers gone, either in an ambulance or a police car.

It made Aldric aware that this was far from the end, though. They'd solved the case but set so much more in motion. Randa Buckman would be charged with several crimes, which would make the news. He sighed.

"We should go." Darrell stepped down and helped Aldric down too, holding his hand for longer than was necessary. Aldric couldn't resist smiling his thanks, and Darrell returned it. *Oh.* Aldric's heart squeezed again and he wondered how long the seeds of love actually took to sprout...and if they'd taken root at first sight, after all.

"Wait," Elliot said, holding up a hand. The other held something he was refusing to let a police officer take. "Before you go and before this is taken into custody or evidence or whatever, don't you think we should have a final chance to open it? To solve it, Aldric?" He passed what he carried to him.

Aldric was sick of the sight of the Buckman artifacts, this one especially, and almost dropped the puzzle box. "Me? I tried. We all did, remember?"

"Darrell didn't," Elliot pointed out, nodding at him. "Let him try."

"I don't know anything about these things!" Darrell protested to Elliot. "I couldn't even solve a Rubik's Cube." Still, he took the puzzle from Aldric and held it up to catch the light, then turned it around, examining it from all angles and sides.

"You think it's the inlay squares that hold the key?" Aldric asked Elliot, who nodded. He stared at the hexagonal box in Darrell's hands. The pale blue of the police vehicle light played over it, giving it a macabre appearance.

"These are different colors, right?" Darrell said at last. "I mean, I know they're white, not brown like the wood. I remember that from seeing the box before. But are some of them yellower than the others?"

"I think so!" Aldric put a hand around the box, so he and Darrell held it together, one hand each, their free hands touching. "They make a pattern, I think? They go up in a curve around the side here, to the middle of the back and up over the top to stop in the middle of what could be the lid here..."

"And the same on this side, to meet in the center of the lid. And see what the shape is?" Darrell asked.

Aldric studied the curvature his fingers were making, and the identical one Darrel's hand was curled into. "It's a heart," he whispered. "Isn't it?"

"Looks like it. Shall we try?"

"Yes. Even though we don't know for sure, and we might get it wrong, we should try." Aldric brushed the back of his hand against Darrell's, trusting that Darrell understood the question and that his answer had been about far more than the puzzle. They were gathering an audience.

"On three? Elliot, count us in?" Darrell suggested.

On Elliot's *three*, with everyone standing close and holding their breaths, Aldric and Darrell touched their fingertips to the off-white inlaid squares that felt cooler to Aldric than the wood of the box—and nothing happened. They stopped, together. "Elliot?" Aldric asked.

"Try again," came his suggestion, and he began the count.

Still nothing happened.

"I'll count," Darrell said, and they did it again.

"Anything?" Sean asked, with a sidelong glance at the other patrol officers. "Only they really need to get to the station and process all this in."

"I know!" Darrell snapped. "Aldric, you say go."

"Go?" Aldric said, and he and Darrell pressed the tips of their fingers onto the ivory squares. "Nothing!" he exclaimed.

"Maybe nothing's right." Darrell dropped his hand from the box. "As in, there is nothing. Or it's something else that opens it. Either way, we can't keep doing this all damn night."

"Hmm. I wonder." Elliot coughed. "How many times have you tried that move?"

Aldric frowned. "Four." He turned the box around in his hand, feeling its hexagon shape. *Hexagon. Five!* "So we should do it again! Darrell, five! On three, go. One, two—"

"*Three.*" Darrell finished the count and pressed in perfect symmetry with Aldric, and the box lid slid open. Everyone gasped and half of their audience cheered. "Grab that thing inside it," he ordered and Aldric plunged his fingers in and snatched the many-folded sheet of paper out.

Before anyone could stop him, he smoothed the paper flat. After all they'd been through, he had to know. The tiny writing was difficult to make out, but he managed, and drew Darrell's attention to what Buck Buckman had left his son. It was more than just the house. "No wonder Randa was worried and tried to retrieve the items she'd sold."

He imagined she'd thought it would be a simple matter of snatching them back and destroying them before anyone found the will, only to discover it wasn't.

"Buckman must have told his son, sent him some hints or messages," Darrell mused. "And his son came to town. Or maybe just for the funeral. Guess we'll find out." He dropped the puzzle box into an evidence bag Sean was holding out and grinned at Aldric. "It's amazing what we can do, if we try together."

* * * *

They were together again for another occasion in which the SAPD was involved, almost a month later. The Buckman funeral had been held, a private ceremony, which his son Nick and the guy he was seeing, Mateo — Darrell's former hook-up — attended, but not his widow, Randa. The case was ongoing, and Darrell had no choice but to be involved, but preferred to focus on other things, such as changes in his career, and him and Aldric.

Like now, at the police substation, in the press briefing room. Captain Miller didn't have as much to say on an occasion like this as Fuentes would have, and the audience was a lot smaller, but Darrell was just as reluctant to step into the spotlight. He did, though.

"Thank you, Captain Miller," he began. "I'm pleased to accept the position of LGBTQ liaison officer for the substation." The enthusiastic applause startled him. This had been a rocky road, but he and Fuentes then he, Fuentes and Miller had hammered it out. "It's the first, I hope, of similar liaison posts to serve culturally specific communities, including minorities and special needs communities." He tried not to smile at Aldric in the audience, mouthing the words along with him. They'd practiced together.

"The last time I was publicly recognized and given an honor here in this room, I was called brave. I didn't feel brave inside, then, though. I do now. I've learned a lot since then about what courage is. I won't give a long speech" — he tried not to look at Fuentes, although Sean snorted in laughter — "but I want to tell anyone who needs to hear it not to be afraid to try, even if it makes you vulnerable, and that *that* is not the same as being weak. Being sensitive to needs, including your own, and needing to care and be cared for, is an honor and a privilege, not a failing or weakness. Thank you."

Elliot and Jonas, on either side of Aldric, stood and applauded with him. Darrell knew the older men, looking a little bemused, were his twin brothers. They were sitting with Brianna, who'd become a friend, and Leah, who was putting her foot down about *'Ryan's family ruling our lives'*. Darrell had the feeling that under Leah's influence, Ryan would make his own decision about whether to be in Darrell's life or not. Best of all, Darrell had been in touch with his mother, wanting to rebuild their relationship, to get to know her away from his father's view of things.

He left the platform and Aldric, handsome in a new suit, met him. "You look so good in your full uniform," he said. "Well, more than good, but I can't tell you here."

"Can you tell me later tonight?" Aldric spent so much time at Darrell's now that he'd practically moved in, and Darrell wanted to talk to him about co-signing the lease with him. Anytime they'd talked about it, Aldric had insisted he'd pay half the rent, but Darrell wanted him to use the salary he made at Intrinsic Value to pay for community college. That Aldric had the confidence to think about studying for his associate degree and was even thinking about one day taking a bachelors at one of the universities in town made Darrell so happy.

"Oh yes." Aldric's brown eyes shone bright. "Do you want me to come over?"

"More than that." Darrell didn't even think, just let the words fall. "I want you to fuck me."

"*What?*" Aldric never had, because Darrell had always topped. *Always.*

"I said—"

"I heard. But"— Aldric waved a hand around the room—"you pick your moments! What, *now?*"

"Well, let's get home first, okay?" Darrell suggested. He'd thought he'd feel nervous, and he did, a little, but the buzz of arousal had him feeling almost high. *And so fucking horny.* And shit, he had the rest of this goddamn event to get through, before he could even think about hightailing it home…

Chapter Twenty-One

It was Darrell's habit to open doors for Aldric and usher Aldric ahead of him, but that evening, with Aldric's cute ass wiggling in front of Darrell, he almost pushed Aldric into his apartment with his cock, which was straining in his jeans.

"Oh." Aldric pressed back a little in that way of his that Darrell was never sure was deliberate or not. "You seem ready to go. Are you sure?"

"Yes." Darrell turned Aldric round. "I know you love me fucking you, but—"

The image of Aldric writhing under him, those beautiful big brown eyes closed tight and his small white teeth biting down on his bottom lip when Darrell penetrated him, robbed Darrell of speech mid-sentence. It also had him weak at the knees. They'd discovered Aldric loved toys almost as much as he loved Darrell's cock—*"and it'd better never be more"*, Darrell had told him gruffly at least twice. Aldric's favorite dildos and vibrators varied from day to day, and Darrell laughed at the cute names Aldric gave them. The blue meanie had been supplanted by the purple monster as Aldric's current fave.

"But I'm ready to get fucked in the ass. If that's okay with you?" Darrell added, deliberately using the kind of language that got Aldric juiced.

They'd discussed it — sort of — as in, it would happen when Darrell was ready, and that maybe Aldric wasn't a switch or a top. "If it's not working for you, we stop. Simple as that," Darrell assured Aldric, stripping his coat from him. Aldric's slim chest in that eggplant-colored button-down, the shade chosen to bring out his deep brown eyes, had Darrell's balls filling.

Aldric dropped his gaze and bent his head in that way he did when he wanted Darrell to come in close. Darrell obliged, and Aldric whispered, "'To get to savor you, to spend as long as I want, as long as you need, getting you ready? Oh, Mama!'"

"Hey!" Darrell objected. "I never said 'Oh, Mama.' When have I ever said 'Oh, Mama'? And if you reply, 'You will tonight', I'll…" He couldn't go on for laughing. Sex with Aldric was both earth-shattering and life-affirming.

"Don't worry," Aldric continued, and it took him adding, "'You're gonna love this. Be begging for more. Wondering how you got through life without a cock up your ass,'" for Darrell to catch on that the sly little bastard was still quoting his words back at him. "But why now?"

"What can I say?" Darrell shrugged. "The heart wants what the heart wants."

"It's not exactly the *heart* we're talking about, though, is it?" Aldric's eyes gleamed.

"I'm giving you a head start of five." Darrell raised an eyebrow. "Then that cheeky ass of yours is gettin' spanked."

Laughing and calling for mercy, Aldric raced to the bathroom. He was half-naked when Darrell got there, having peeled off some clothes on the way, and Darrell helped him with the rest, cupping his balls just to see how quickly he could make Aldric's cock fill. Darrell started the water and motioned for Aldric to go first. Showering together was something they both liked, exchanging long, slow kisses and caresses under the hot water, wreathed in the steam that rose all around them, Darrell finding new spots to bite Aldric and make him squeal with the sound going straight to Darrell's dick.

This evening, he bent his head to give a quick bite to Aldric's nipple, then a lengthier suck of the distended flesh.

"I think I'd want rings," Aldric murmured.

It took Darrell a nano-second to flick to an ongoing conversation of theirs about Aldric getting piercings. "And they'd look fuckin' sexy. Wash me?" As much as he loved taking care of Aldric, today he wanted Aldric lathering up his hands and spreading foamy soap on him, because he had a surprise for him.

Aldric started by washing his hair, scratching his nails into Darrell's crew-cut that he was letting grow a little longer, and making Darrell moan when he massaged his temples. He couldn't stand still, couldn't be passive, so grabbed himself a palmful of body wash to spread on Aldric's neck and shoulders, catching the run-off to rub in small circles into Aldric's fine underarm hair.

As always, every touch got them both harder and more eager for the other until they could no longer pretend they were doing anything but rubbing up against each other, their caresses becoming increasingly shorter and harder strokes, just as their kisses went from leisurely to desperate. Darrell slowed things down. He didn't want them getting off like that, not tonight.

He turned, his hands against the glass of the cubicle and leaned forward slightly, but enough for Aldric to exclaim in surprise at the butt plug Darrell was wearing. Darrell could feel all the questions beating inside Aldric's mind. Could Aldric pick the answers from Darrell's…?

Yes, he'd been wearing the plug all afternoon and early evening, adding more lube as necessary.

Yes, it hit his prostate if he got the angle and position right. *Jesus*, just like the way Aldric was moving it in his tentative exploration.

Yes, he was preparing himself to take Aldric's dick, and yes, it was making him horny.

Aldric whispered a question, and Darrell nodded, granting permission. A second later, Aldric's fingers tickled around the flared base and pulled to ease the plug loose. Darrell teased Aldric a little, clenching his sphincter muscles to make Aldric work to free the toy. He peeped over his shoulder to see Aldric examining the bulbous black rubber with curiosity.

"You've used one," Darrell reminded him.

"Not this size." Aldric's voice was almost lost under the cascading water.

The plug wasn't *that* big. Darrell wanted to feel Aldric taking him and the effects of his penetration as long into tomorrow as they lasted. The toy was bigger, though, than the slim starter one he'd eased into Aldric the first time they'd had sex without condoms. Aldric had wanted to hold Darrell's cum inside him as long as he could, so Darrell had inserted a butt plug after they'd fucked, and Aldric had slept with it in.

Darrell had pressed into it while curled around Aldric, being the big spoon, and the moan Aldric had given in his sleep when the tip pressed on his prostate was a sound Darrell would never forget. Now, he relished the slight looseness of his sphincter and smiled when Aldric unhooked the showerhead and sluiced his ass.

"Is there any point to that when you'll be getting me dirty again?" Darrell wondered.

"'Don't wanna be tasting soap in a few, do I?'" Aldric said in a deeper, gruffer tone than his usual one.

"It's like living with a goddamn parrot," Darrell complained of Aldric's mimicking him. Again. He switched off the water and opened the door for Aldric to exit. Outside, he twisted a towel into a strip and slapped it against the clothes hamper meaningfully, his eyes narrowed, and his mouth set into a thin line.

His fake threat and just-as-fake scowl worked, because with a squeal, Aldric fled, still patting himself dry. He'd gone to the bedroom. Darrell wrapped a towel around his waist and followed. He snagged a spare towel as he exited, because Aldric never rubbed his hair dry enough by Darrell's standards, and today was no exception.

Aldric submitted to having his fluffy brown hair toweled and asked, "Are you stalling?"

"Not exactly. But, Aldric…"

"What?"

"Be gentle with me." Standing close to Aldric, close enough to feel his breath on his skin, Darrell let Aldric see that while the words sounded flippant, in line with the humor that made up a big part of their relationship, the request was real. That Darrell stood before him, defenses down, vulnerable.

"Always," Aldric promised, his voice catching. He patted the bed, and Darrell lay down for Aldric to follow and drop slow, sensual kisses on him, kisses so sweet and yet so scorching that they could only have come from Aldric.

Darrell stretched out under him, turning his head into Aldric's hand where it rested in his hair and pushing into the warmth of Aldric's fingers sliding from his hip to cup his ass.

He breathed out a half-giggle when Aldric nuzzled into his neck, then took a nip of his collarbone. Aldric pulled away to lean over to the nightstand for the lube.

"Okay?" Aldric murmured, perhaps not so much a question as in response to Darrell turning onto his stomach and curling his arms around his pillow.

He nodded, feeling Aldric's body heat a second before Aldric nudged his thighs apart to kneel between them, his torso curved over Darrell's back and shoulders. "I'll go slowly," he promised.

Darrell nodded again and breathed out at the touch of a wet finger at his hole. Aldric pushed it gradually inward, the firm probe hesitant and sensuous. And addictive—Darrell's knees straightened under him so he could arch upward a little, giving Aldric more access. Within seconds, Aldric was past the first ring of muscle.

"Stay still," he said, and Darrell, despite craving more, tried, except when he had to turn his face, still buried in the pillow, to one side so he could breathe his anticipation out, instead of pushing back onto Aldric's hand to assuage it.

"I said I was taking this slowly," Aldric whispered in his ear before he dipped lower, to kiss what little of Darrell's face was visible and touchable. "This is amazing, how you feel, so tough and tender at the same time. Did you know I've been fantasizing about being inside you?"

It wasn't what anyone would consider filthy, and certainly not the kind of dirty talk Darrell loosed during sex and got Aldric so goddam horny that he moaned where he lay, stroking his cock and cradling his balls, demanding Darrell take him, *now*. And Jesus, how Darrell loved seeing Aldric come undone like that. *Love undoing him.* But the fact that it was Aldric, with his bouncy brown hair and doe-like eyes, saying such a thing here, now—it had Darrell seeking out Aldric's lips and pushing upward and backward, onto his hand.

But only for Aldric to use his body weight to hold him down to continue opening him up at his own pace. Darrell felt every millimeter of the second finger Aldric added, felt it in the increased pressure and stretch it brought. The hum of satisfaction Aldric gave resonated through his chest to Darrell, tickling his ear. Aldric twisting and turning his fingers had Darrell moaning— some of it in frustration.

"Give me more," he urged with a shake of his hips. "Not like I haven't taken anything in the ass before, remember?"

Aldric nipped Darrell's ear, and the tiny bite sent tremors along Darrell's skin. "This isn't just about you. I'll never have this first experience with you again. Not like this. So let me take my time and enjoy you."

It might have come out as a plea if he hadn't trailed his mouth around to that spot behind Darrell's ear that drove him wild when Aldric bit it—as he was now, increasing the pressure until Darrell shivered. Aldric twisted the fingers he had buried inside him, stretching him further, then added a third.

Darrell forced himself to relax and accept the stretch and sting. He couldn't hold in the moan of appreciation when Aldric twisted his wrist, sliding deeper and using his thumb to stroke the outer ring of muscles. Darrell's cock wanted in on the action now but was trapped, rock hard and throbbing, under him. He flexed his hips, rutting against the sheets, and apprehension turned his moan sharper when Aldric glided his fingers out then replaced them with the head of his cock.

"Ready?" Aldric asked, his voice low and almost steady.

Darrell didn't hesitate as heat raced through his body, surging with anticipation. "Yes. Please, please give me—"

The breath was stolen from him when Aldric pressed forward, breaching the tight ring in one deliberate push. Sweat coated Darrell's skin and he clenched his eyes shut against the burn and pressure, and when that wasn't enough, pushed his face once more into the pillow, to blot any tears and muffle any sounds of protest. Aldric made soothing noises when Darrell's body stiffened, despite his efforts—his instinctive reaction to getting his ass fucked.

"Come here."

It took him a second to understand, to turn his head to where Aldric's voice spoke, and when he did it was to meet his gaze. It took Aldric's tongue poking at Darrell's teeth to make him realize he was biting down on his lower lip. Darrell inhaled, deep and slow, letting himself sink into the burn in his ass. Aldric managed to kiss him, in that twisted-over position, and Darrell opened to him—in all senses—sucking on his tongue and pushing upward to take more of Aldric's thick cock deep inside him.

"I'm all the way inside you."

Inside me. The psychological weight anchored him, and he absorbed the physical impact a heartbeat later, when Aldric rocked gently within him, barely moving, then pulled out so just the tip of his dick sat inside Darrell's still-tight, still-resisting ass. Then what Darrell could see of Aldric's face contorted in pleasure when he plunged in once more, hard, sending too many sensations through Darrell to chart them. It only took two or three thrusts for any residual pain and discomfort to swirl and mix into pleasure, making his world nothing but heat and pressure and Aldric.

"Babe, angle that way." Darrell shifted his hips to show him, then failed to hold in his cry when Aldric's dick rubbed over his prostate. The next few thrusts had Darrell jerking like a puppet with Aldric pulling his strings. He didn't think Aldric would last, not with the way he was clenching hot and tight around Aldric, spasming as his channel and his cock, still imprisoned under him, were worked mercilessly.

"Darrell, I can't—" Aldric's lunges became erratic and he thrust deeper than before, banging so fiercely against Darrell's ass that a guttural shout was torn from him as pleasure enveloped him. His climax hit him without warning. He arched into Aldric's next thrust, his world reduced to the white roar in his ears, and every nerve sizzled with fire while his untouched cock pulsed and spent. He gripped the sheet under him, his fingers clawing hard.

Aldric pushed in, deep and deliberate. "Darrell!" he shouted as he came, then loosed a hoarse string of expletives. Aldric's release, the hot throb of semen inside Darrell, was the most intimate thing he'd ever felt.

Darrell needed the silence and stillness that followed, and Aldric still lying connected to him. When Aldric pulled out, his torso slipping off Darrell's sweaty skin, the loss of sensation had Darrell aching all over. That was a different pain from the more localized throb in his ass. Did Aldric have his face buried in the pillow too, Darrell wondered, once his heart stopped its thundering and his brain started up again so he could form thoughts. Now that he could move, he closed his legs to trap Aldric's between them and wriggled his hand that rested in the middle of him and Aldric, for Aldric to seek out and grasp.

They lay quietly for a while, fastened together while the sweat and cum cooled on their bodies, then laughed when they both moved at the same time, to curl onto their sides to face the other. They moved in unison again, to get close enough to kiss, both too exhausted to exchange more than tiny touches of their lips. When Darrell pulled back, he searched Aldric's face, just as Aldric was examining his.

"Was that..." Aldric peeked up at him through his eyelashes in that coy way Darrell found endearing. It also made him want to throw Aldric down and screw him stupid. Even now, his cock, drained limp, sticky, tried to stir at the sight and the idea. "...all right?" Aldric finished.

"All— *Jesus*! I can't move, so what do you think?" Darrell exclaimed. He caught the giggle that bubbled through Aldric. "You liked that." He didn't make it a question. "Liked fucking me."

"No." Aldric's tiny head shake worried Darrell, for half a second. "I *loved* it. But I'm confused." He blinked, wide-eyed, but Darrell wasn't falling for it. "I don't know which I prefer."

"No problem. I'll fuck you, soon as I've recovered, and you can compare," Darrell started to say, but Aldric's rumbling stomach drowned out his words, making Darrell realize he was hungry too, and that they'd skipped dinner.

Annoyed at himself for not taking better care of Aldric, Darrell grabbed the towel he'd dropped to the floor and cleaned them both up. "C'mon. Let's hunt up some supper." He stood carefully, his ass throbbing. *Good.*

The fridge contained enough shredded lettuce, grated carrots and sliced tomatoes to make a bowl of salad, into which he tipped some cubes of cheese. He turned to see Aldric stretch for a bag of marshmallows behind the jars on a shelf then grab a pair of scissors and run their blades under the faucet to wet them and make the candy easier to cut.

Darrell narrowed his eyes at Aldric's proficient, practiced move *and* at him having snuck crap into their would-be-healthy kitchen. When Aldric snipped the pink and white cubes into smaller squares and let them fall into the salad, Darrell couldn't contain himself any longer.

"I love you."

Aldric stirred the contents of the bowl. "Yes, I know."

Darrell frowned. "Babe, you're supposed to say—"

"I love you too." Aldric gave that more sly than shy grin at having tricked Darrell. *Again.* And held out a fork, on which he'd speared tomato, cheese and marshmallow, for him to taste.

"Good."

"Good?" Aldric echoed, looking at the empty fork.

Darrell swallowed the forkful. "Not that, no. Jesus, it's vile. But, good. As in, this is good. Life is good."

It was. He picked out a bit of candy for Aldric and fed him with his fingers. He thought of that odd little antiques store, a place of one-offs, both items and people, and how it had brought Aldric into his life.

Where Darrell would work hard every day to keep him.

Want to see more from this author?
Here's a taster for you to enjoy!

Something Shattered
Bailey Bradford

Excerpt

Jesse Martin sat on the porch steps of his rented trailer, looking at the sparse patches of grass in his tiny yard. The New Mexico sun was bright in the clear blue sky, the heat beyond oppressive and bordering on hellish.

The beer bottle in his hand was sweating almost as much as he was, and he wondered if the yellowish-brown color of the grass meant it was dead or just severely dehydrated. Maybe if he watered the grass, it would eventually become a lush green carpet like his neighbor's. That was one pretty lawn across the street.

Right. Like he would remember to water the pathetic splotch that was his yard—and he sure didn't want to know what that would do to his water bill. If the landlady didn't like the crappy lawn, then *she* could foot the bill and take care of the stuff. At least this way he didn't have to mow.

Still, he couldn't help but be a little envious of that thick, green grass across the street. The neighbor must be some kind of plant-life miracle worker. Even the man's back yard was flourishing. It was possible that he had an in-ground sprinkler system or something, which was well beyond Jesse's means.

Jesse took a drink of his warm beer. *Still nasty*. If he were smart, he'd sit out here with a little ice chest, though even then he'd have to really chug the beer to get it down before the temperature did a number on it.

Glancing at his watch, he saw it was five till three. He turned his attention to the house across the street. From behind darkly tinted sunglasses, he watched, waiting for the door to that home to open. A ripple of anticipation went through him.

Sure enough, as had happened Monday through Saturday every afternoon for the past month, the door slowly opened.

Jesse's anticipation doubled. He tensed, waiting for what would happen next. When he saw it, he slumped with relief. Nothing had changed today.

One thin arm slipped out of the opened door, inch by inch.

Then, Jesse's heart did its usual odd skippy-thing that happened every time he watched.

A man appeared, cautiously moving through the doorway. Beat-up tennis shoes, baggy denim jeans, a ratty T-shirt about two sizes too big for his frame, a cast on his lower right arm that had gotten dingier since Jesse had first seen it. Everything the neighbor had on was pretty much the same outfit Jesse had seen before. Whether this was due to the guy having a bunch of the same shirts, bad hygiene, or a limited wardrobe, Jesse hadn't a clue. It wasn't like he could just ask either — they weren't exactly on speaking terms.

After only a few seconds' hesitation, the man moved through the doorway and stepped onto the little cement porch. Jesse checked him out as inconspicuously as possible. Not quite short, and thin to the point of gauntness, the man was a mystery to everyone in the small town of El Jardin. Tongues were wagging, and gossip spreading. Some of the stories people told were unbelievable and, to Jesse, solid proof that the creators of those tales had too much time on their hands.

Besides, he remembered very clearly what it was like to be the new kid in town, even though ten years had passed. Jesse still wasn't completely accepted by all the natives. More than a few of them talked about him, but he ignored them. For some reason, that was harder to do when the gossiping was about his new neighbor. Even his coworker, Officer Pat Monroe, made remarks here and there. But that didn't surprise Jesse. Monroe was an asshole who never missed an opportunity to make snide remarks. Some days it seemed Monroe spent more time talking trash than performing his duties as a police officer.

Jesse tried not to give such talk any credence, with the exception of ensuring there wasn't some pervert living across the street. No, he'd rather get the truth from the source, but that was kind of hard to do when the source wasn't talking.

Granted, Jesse hadn't tried too hard, just knocked on the door the day after the guy had moved in. When his knock had gone unanswered, he'd figured his new neighbor was either asleep or maybe at a doctor's appointment, considering all the injuries he'd had. Jesse had walked back to his trailer and gotten ready for work. Right before getting in his car to leave, he'd glanced across and noticed that a printed sign now graced the door. Curious, Jesse had walked to the sidewalk, squinting in an attempt to read it.

DO NOT DISTURB THE TENANT.

Well. That had seemed pretty clear. Jesse hadn't been offended by the snotty sign at the time. Easy enough to understand, since the man was so banged up. Except, over a month later, the sign was still up. Pretty clear, but not so understandable. *Now* the sign just seemed rude.

Jesse took another drink of his beer, grimacing as the heated liquid hit his tongue. The neighbor was at the mailbox now. Well, not exactly *at* the mailbox — that would mean he had to step off the sidewalk and into the street. Instead, as was the norm on these little treks, he kept his feet firmly planted on the edge of the walkway while he leaned forward and stretched out his left hand to retrieve the mail. *Probably not uncomfortable, Jesse mused, but still, why not just take the few extra steps to actually* walk *to the mailbox?*

The man slapped the box lid shut and pivoted carefully. Jesse quit trying to pretend he wasn't watching and tipped his glasses down. Without the dark tint impeding his vision, he was treated to a brilliant display of gorgeous, curly auburn hair. The sun brought out streaks of red as well as glints of gold and orange in the silky-looking mess. Jesse's fingers tightened on the beer bottle — the urge to touch the colorful curls was nearly a physical thing.

He sat on the steps for several minutes after the neighbor had disappeared back inside, wondering how pathetic he'd become when this was the highlight of his day.

Caleb took a deep breath and steeled himself. He could do this, *he could.* It was a pretty sorry thing when a grown man had to work to find the courage to walk fifteen feet to his own mailbox. Some days it took longer than others to even open the door.

Maybe that cop will be sitting on his steps. He'd seen the man numerous times — there were times it made his trip outside easier, knowing there was a police officer just a few feet away. Sometimes it made him nervous, though, because Caleb was pretty sure the guy was watching him. Maybe it was all innocuous, or maybe the cop was watching him for other reasons. Did he think Caleb was a criminal, some kind of threat to the people in this town?

Caleb actually snorted at the idea as he made himself unlock the deadbolts then slip on the glasses. His fingers shook as he reached for the doorknob, but he managed to turn it with a slight twist of the wrist. Caleb gingerly opened the door, fighting to keep his muscles from trembling. A deep breath, then another, and he was able to take the step that brought him outside and onto his porch.

I can do this. Keeping his head down, Caleb willed his feet to move. Slowly, he shuffled down the sidewalk. The sun's heat seemed to seep inside him, warming the dark, frightened places in his mind. Caleb tipped his head up just enough to see the man sitting on his porch. He looked big and fit, a tight T-shirt clinging to sculpted muscles. *Safe. I'm safe as long as he's out here too.*

Caleb stopped at the edge of the sidewalk, fighting against the flush that crawled up his cheeks. *Why can't I take even one step off it?* The very idea made his heart race erratically, pound so hard he wondered if he might have a heart attack. *Just check the damn mail!* Caleb reached for the mailbox lid, not thinking until that moment just how bizarre his ritual must seem to an observer.

No wonder he watches me. I'm a damned freak. He dared a glance at the man. Now he was certain the guy was watching. Caleb fumbled as he grasped at the mail, his fingers not cooperating, hands shaking a little. Bending forward more, he managed to grab the envelopes and pull them from the box. Caleb slapped the lid shut and turned back to his house. He would not peek over his shoulder, he *wouldn't*. And he wouldn't run either.

It took all his concentration to keep his steps slow and steady, embarrassment and shame pushing at him as he felt the man's gaze prickling his spine. By the time he was back inside, the deadbolts firmly in place, Caleb's nerves were shot. He wondered how much longer he could go on the way he'd been doing the past month or so. *Will I always be this fucked up?* He didn't really want an answer to that because he knew it'd just depress him.

Caleb called his puppy to him. "Loopy! Come snuggle."

The adorable toy poodle came bounding into the room, and leaped up onto the couch where Caleb had sprawled. "Good baby." There was nothing like puppy kisses and cuddles to take his mind off unpleasant things.

* * * *

Inside the stuffy trailer, Jesse shrugged out of his clothes and pulled a uniform from the closet. As he dressed for work, he couldn't stop thinking about his neighbor. The man's odd behavior and general unfriendliness were reasons enough, in his opinion, to keep an eye on the guy. Add to that his mysterious arrival in the wee hours of the morning weeks ago, and Jesse couldn't help but be curious.

It was possible that a lot of people moved into a new place at three in the morning, but it seemed strange to him. He supposed it also played into the mystery about the neighbor, ensuring Jesse would continue watching him, working it all over in his mind.

He'd never seen the man at the store or anywhere out in public. Chances were, in such a small town, they would have run into each other at the local grocery store at the very least. The guy had to be getting food somewhere, unless he was stocked up in preparation for doomsday. He wouldn't be the only one in El Jardin to do so.

Jesse did glean some things about his neighbor, like that he must be a sucker for animals, because there was a yappy dog in the big back yard sometimes. There was also a gray tabby cat that was, as far as Jesse could tell, more than a little on the feral side. The few times he'd tried to approach the cat had resulted in the tabby bolting for cover. Still, he'd seen the animal crouched on the porch, nibbling away at a pile of cat food. The free meals didn't put a dent in the tabby's hunting stints. Jesse was pretty sure the cat was responsible for the deaths of a quarter of the local bird population, despite the meals his neighbor provided.

Is the guy just crazy, though? Or is he suffering from the aftereffects of whatever violent event happened to him before he moved here?

More fuel had been added to the fire last week when Jesse had overheard Lisa down at the tax office talking about how the house had been purchased in a woman's name. Shannon, Lisa's coworker, had pointed out that her sister worked for the utility company, and those too had been put in a woman's name. It had been on the tip of Jesse's tongue to inform them they were sharing information that, by law, they shouldn't have, but he *had* listened. Besides, a scolding from him wouldn't have stopped them anyway, and it'd just have made Jesse look like a prick.

All these things pushed Jesse to find some answers. The truth was, on the off chance someone had personally assaulted his neighbor... Well, it would be better for the neighbor if Jesse knew that, even if the person responsible were in jail. If it was some sort of accident, maybe he could drop a hint about that here and there around town, try to turn the tide of small-town disapproval. Nothing major, just some basis for telling the wagging tongues to back off.

Was he going a little too far with his determination to find out more about the man? If he was, he wasn't alone. There were enough people in the dinky town just waiting and watching, wondering what the *odd* new guy in El Jardin was doing. At least Jesse only wanted to know because his cop senses were tingling. He had no intention of spreading gossip. And it had absolutely nothing to do with the fact that he found himself oddly attracted to the man.

PUBLISHING

Sign up for our newsletter and find out about all our romance book releases, eBook sales and promotions, sneak peeks and FREE romance books!

About the Author

A native Texan, Bailey spends her days spinning stories around in her head, which has contributed to more than one incident of tripping over her own feet. Evenings are reserved for pounding away at the keyboard, as are early morning hours. Sleep? Doesn't happen much. Writing is too much fun, and there are too many characters bouncing about, tapping on Bailey's brain demanding to be let out.

Caffeine and chocolate are permanent fixtures in Bailey's office and are never far from hand at any given time. Removing either of those necessities from Bailey's presence can result in what is known as A Very, Very Scary Bailey and is not advised under any circumstances.

Bailey loves to hear from readers. You can find her contact information, website details and author profile page at https://www.pride-publishing.com